# The
# Marvelous
# Palace

# The
# MARVELOUS
# PALACE

## and Other Stories

# PIERRE BOULLE

*Translated by Margaret Giovanelli*

THE VANGUARD PRESS, INC.
NEW YORK

Library of Congress Catalogue Card Number: 77-0629
ISBN: 0-8149-0788-1

Designer: Elizabeth Woll
Manufactured in the United States of America.

# Contents

$T$HE OLD MAN who told me these stories professes to be a priest, but he is a minister of no recognized faith. His religion, he said at the time of our first meeting, is the religion of Doubt. This word he pronounced emphatically. When I asked for enlightenment, he replied that his doctrine could not be taught but should be approached cautiously. He let me understand, however, that he would provide me with some illustrations when we were better acquainted, if I had the patience to listen to him. But he was by no means sure this could satisfy a stripling like me.

Because I smiled at this word applied to myself, he informed me he was a centenarian. I don't know whether this particular is correct, for he is apt to stretch the truth; in any case, he is very old. He expresses himself with a refined politeness, even with preciosity, punctuating most of his sentences and often beginning them with "Monsieur." As for me, I was unable to address him without taking the precaution of paying homage to his great age, and I responded liberally with "Old Man," which, in the country from which he comes, was a title of courtesy used in his day in speaking to an ancient. For even though his exact nationality seems to me as hazy as his religion and his age, there is no doubt he is Asian. He resembles Hindus, Chinese, and Malays. Whenever he speaks of his country, he calls it pompously the Kingdom of Shandong. I thought it must be a very small state situated somewhere in the Himalayan massif. But I've never been much interested in geographical details and have never asked him to pinpoint the fact.

At times he wanders a bit in speaking of recent events, but his recollection seems quite faithful in recalling old memories, and his stories have held my attention. He loves the bizarre for its own sake and I would not be the one to reproach him for this.

He also seems to be somewhat lacking in feeling, sometimes taking a perverse pleasure in certain curious, even sinister, adventures without seeming to attach the slightest importance to the pain the vagaries of destiny may cause their targets. I suspect him of putting this love of the unusual (which takes the place of aesthetic feeling among certain less favored beings) well ahead of charity and the other virtues one would expect to find in a man of religious vocation, even though he be a minister of Doubt.

Is he wholly wanting in humanity? I cannot tell. Now and again he is capable of displaying a degree of emotion. Or of feigning it. Certainly there is a tinge of charlatanry mixed with cynicism in him. In fact, I often wonder whether he is not an incarnation of the Devil.

In short, in some respects he resembles me like a brother. He is one of those whose company I seek on the evenings when, driven to despair by the frightful clichés the Western world offers the professional storyteller, sickened by the banality of personal experience and having taken a meritorious but imprudent oath never again to make use of such subjectivity in my writing, I would willingly abandon my soul to the Demon in exchange for an original idea.

# The
# Royal
# Pardon

$T$HE OLD MAN WAS seated opposite me in the almost always deserted, dusty café, where I was in the habit of drawing him out when he felt in the mood to tell his beads of memory. He began thus in his characteristically pompous tone:

"Monsieur, the story I propose to tell you this evening, if you have the desire and courtesy to listen, illustrates in a quite remarkable way a virtue much honored in the Kingdom of Shandong, a virtue whose roots plunge into prehistory and that has been piously preserved for generations. I wish to speak of love."

I could scarcely conceal a slight grimace. Love seems to me like a literary terrain spaded up, sown thousands of times, and impoverished to the point where it is impossible today to make new flowers blossom. Then he added:

"To be precise, Monsieur, it has to do with maternal love."

I had even greater difficulty in concealing my disillusion, so deep-seated in me is the idea that the finest sentiments never beget good literature—a noble thought I read somewhere long ago. However, I said to myself I might just as well waste my evening listening to his story, commonplace though it might be, as in wandering mindlessly through the streets in a doubtless futile search for a provocative subject.

"Women, Monsieur, play an essential role in this story."

"I'm all ears, Old Man," I said. And, to myself, I'll be patient.

"Monsieur, I shall recount the steps of the adventure in the manner in which I lived through the events, for I was closely involved in them.

"I shall begin with the interview the Queen of Shandong granted to the young lawyer I was at that time. Indeed, I had not yet renounced the world and I was a lawyer with only a few years of experience, but I was full of good will and had summoned all my strength, all my juridical knowledge and my modest eloquence to plead one last time before our sovereign the cause of an unfortunate young man who had just been condemned to death.

"You should bear in mind, Monsieur, that the Kingdom of Shandong, though isolated from the rest of the

14

world by its high mountains, at that distant epoch was in the vanguard of innovation on which the most progressive nations of the West pride themselves today. We possessed an excellent code of laws, which I hope to give you some glimpses of at a later occasion, and our wise Constitution had established the absolute equality of the rights of man and woman, with the possibility that a woman might accede to all governmental functions, including the highest offices of State. As a result, some months earlier a woman had been chosen Queen of Shandong.

"This had not taken place without lively opposition from reactionaries who deemed a woman to be lacking in *sang-froid* and the necessary objectivity to preside over the destinies of the state. But the modernists carried the day, and the comportment of the Queen, the cleverness, the firm yet supple way in which she governed the kingdom, seemed to justify them. From every point of view she was a remarkable woman: wise, just, possessed of broad culture, and beloved of the people.

"Moreover, a law comparable to one of yours gave the head of state the power to grant as a last resort a free pardon to the unfortunate man condemned by the judges to the supreme punishment. This explains my presence that day before the sovereign."

"Continue, Old Man," I said, already impatient at that long parenthesis. "Now, there you are, facing your Queen, prepared to plead the cause of your client."

"A hapless young man who deserved to live. I do not say that because he was my client. The sentence had been judged excessive by expert jurists and public opinion

15

alike. In fact, there was still doubt that he should have been brought before the court at all, and even if the guilt of murder were admitted, both numerous and powerful attenuating circumstances, as you would say, pleaded in his favor. I could set forth the twists and turns of the crime and the details of the trial, but that would add nothing to the interest of the story."

"Then don't, I beg you; I take you at your word. If the Queen was the wise, just woman you have described, your task should have been quite easy."

"Many of my colleagues thought so. As for me, in spite of a very understandable nervousness, since this was my first such case, I nourished a great hope that had become clearly defined just before I was led into the royal office: The Queen's private secretary, a woman I knew well because once we had pursued legal studies together, had whispered to me that the Queen was well disposed toward my client and in all probability would grant a pardon.

"There I was before the sovereign, a woman of about fifty, though she appeared much younger, with conventional features barely marked by a few wrinkles—traces of her long, studious vigils—who had often shown that her heart was open to pity as long as there was nothing contrary to the interests of state, a characteristic that only strengthened my confidence.

" 'I am listening,' she said to me simply after a courteous reception.

"I began my plea and felt she was indeed listening with sustained attention. Sometimes she would interrupt, and her brief remarks showed she had a thorough knowledge of the condemned man's record. After having perceived

16

certain nods of approval that punctuated my arguments, I had good reason to think my case had been won.

"I had nearly finished and was preparing to sum up when I was disagreeably surprised by the ring of a telephone, which resounded through the office. Monsieur, I know it will seem irrational to you, but I was immediately seized with panic."

The Old Man stopped speaking, and he looked troubled. This feeling, which I had often observed when he was remembering the past, expressed itself not only by the accentuated furrowing of his wrinkles but also by a sudden flush of his whole head. The reaction seemed out of all proportion to a harmless incident. Have I mentioned that I suspect him of being something of an actor? Which, I may say, would not displease me. Aware that so far his recital had left me fairly indifferent, he undoubtedly wished by his facial expression to indicate the moment had arrived for me to shake off my apathy. I played his little game and encouraged him by manifesting the liveliest curiosity.

"Why the panic, Old Man? Isn't it normal for a head of state to receive telephonic communication?"

"Not at all normal, Monsieur. And when I entered her office, the Queen had instructed her secretary that under no circumstances was she to be disturbed during our meeting."

"And the secretary had disobeyed? It must have been for an event of unusual importance."

"So it seemed to me at that moment. Monsieur, I cannot emphasize too strongly what an impression that call made on me. I had the sudden intuition that it was a sign

of dire fate relating to the case I was defending. An un-
reasonable intuition, of course, for there could have been
ten banal explanations. I searched feverishly to conjure
up some, but I could not believe in them: a switchboard
error or an event requiring the Queen's immediate intervention, such as the outbreak of a revolution or the
declaration of an unforeseen war by a neighboring state,
or some quite different national catastrophe—surely grave
crises, the announcement of which I would have received
with perfect serenity in the mental state I was in. That
telephone ring, Monsieur, resounded in my heart like the
death knell of my client."

You know how to prolong the suspense, you old ham,
I grumbled to myself. . . . "Then what was the call
about?"

"You shall learn a little later, as I did. But at that point
I had no knowledge, though certain of the Queen's phrases
should have put me on the track. I should mention that
the Queen herself had been startled by the brutal interruption and seemed as agitated as I. Visibly apprehensive,
she held the receiver nervously and listened a moment in
silence. I surmised that the secretary was explaining to
her why she had dared trouble her. Her facial expression
changed even more as she replied:

" 'You have done well. Put him through to me. . . .
Yes, doctor . . . serious?'

"It was a physician, Monsieur. She listened to the message for what seemed a long time. Her breast rose and fell
in labored breathing, but the marks of emotion that had
ravaged her face diminished little by little. This was truly

a woman of exceptional character. She frowned, thinking hard. It was in an almost composed voice that she asked:

" 'What do you mean by urgent? A few months? A few weeks?'

"She knit her brows again when she heard the answer, and she repeated in an accent of despair:

" 'A few days!'

"Then she regained her self-control.

" 'And you think there's no other way? . . . I understand.'

"Another silence while she listened. I made myself as small as possible in my chair to avoid looking at her. Yet out of the corner of my eye I risked doing so, stirred by the disagreeable impression that her eyes were fixed on me; I was not wrong. She was now watching me with a peculiar expression, one of such intensity that it seemed charged with contained violence, with an insistence that troubled me unutterably and paralyzed me. An impassioned gleam burned in the pupils of her eyes as she stared at me. A little later I was to realize that I was indeed the object of her deep thoughts, or, rather, the personage I represented.

"The Queen's fixed look lasted for a disconcertingly long time; her silence, too. The conversation was interrupted. I no longer heard anything except a slight buzzing in the receiver at regular intervals, doubtless corresponding to a polite questioning by her interlocutor, troubled by her silence. At last the Queen seemed to come out of her hypnotic state and said simply:

" 'That's good, Doctor. You are right to speak to me so

frankly. I shall think about what you have told me and call you back.'

"She hung up the receiver, breathed deeply, made a gesture as if to chase away an importunate thought, and begged me to continue. I myself tried hard to dissipate the painful impression the brusque interruption and her change of attitude had caused in me. I took up the thread of my pleading at the point where I had stopped. As I have told you, there remained nothing further except to recapitulate the motives that had impelled me to solicit the royal pardon. This I did in a few phrases, awkwardly enough, it seemed to me. I was oppressed by the sensation that the atmosphere of the office had grown ominous and that the Queen, favorable to my case an instant before, was now inclined toward a different solution. Oh! she gave no indication of her intentions. She was still listening to me with an appearance of sustained attention, but the attention seemed to me held by a subject quite other than the logic of my arguments. She continued to stare at me in silence, a deep silence that seemed heavy with a disturbing significance, not a single remark showing that she was following the line of my pleading.

"She interrupted me only once, Monsieur. I had finished my summation in a tone I had hoped would be more convincing. I thought fit to conclude by making an appeal to the Queen's heart, this Queen who, on more than one occasion, had shown herself merciful toward her subjects. I alluded to the extreme youth of the condemned, to the despair of his mother, whose only child he was, to the grief of the very old grandparents—arguments without juridical weight, of course, but appropriate to move a sensitive woman. In fact, she seemed to take a new interest in my words and asked:

" 'Very young, you say? How old?'

"That question surprised me. Knowing the brief thoroughly, as she had already given proof, she could not have been ignorant of the condemned man's age. Yet her tone, now commanding, seemed to demand confirmation.

" 'Twenty years old,' I replied.

"She continued in the same imperious tone, as though she were carrying on an inquiry of capital importance to her.

" 'His state of health?'

" 'Excellent, your Majesty. He has maintained complete composure, despite the terrible situation in which he finds himself. Morale sustained by his physical constitution. He has confidence in the justice of his Queen, and that gives him strength. . . .'

"She cut me short with impatience. Quite obviously my last remark did not interest her.

" 'No hidden malady? No family weakness?'

" 'Nothing of that sort, Your Majesty. A healthy lad in every sense. Nothing untoward in his life except this unhappy accident.'

" 'An orphan on his father's side, wasn't he? I read as much in the brief. From infancy? What did his father die of? He must have still been quite young?'

"Monsieur, these feverish questions had more importance than you may suppose. Like you, alas, I could attribute to them no precise significance. I answered:

" 'An accident, Your Majesty. The father was a wood-cutter and was crushed by the fall of a tree.'

" 'The grandparents are very old, you said? How old?'

"I was disconcerted by the odd nature of this inquiry, which seemed to have no bearing on the proceedings. Stammering, I apologized:

" 'I regret not being able to give their exact age, Your Majesty, but I know they are both octogenarians.'

" 'And they are in good health as well as the mother?'

" 'In spite of the blow to this family, they have all over-come their shock with exceptional strength of character.'

"Thus, perceiving that my answers seemed to satisfy the sovereign, I foolishly insisted for several minutes on the physical and moral balance of the members of this family."

"Why foolishly, Old Man? In your place I should have done the same."

"Alas! I was in no position to understand until a little later, and then only to curse myself for having been as unperspicacious as you at this moment. If I had known! But let me go on.

"Our exchange ended on these words. The Queen dismissed me with thanks, declaring that she was going to reflect a bit and that her decision would be made known the next day. I took leave of her, trying, but without success, to persuade myself that I had won the case. I spent a restless night. The next day I was in a state of feverish anxiety when I presented myself at the mother's home in order to be with her when the verdict was announced. Monsieur, I do not wish to keep you in suspense any longer. It is useless to make you endure the frightful hours of waiting we lived through. Contrary to wisdom, contrary to pity, the Queen refused to pardon my wretched client."

My storyteller, the old play-actor, paused again, observing me with eyes glowing like a cat's, bent toward me, visibly awaiting felicitations for the way he was telling his story. I gave him his due with reservations, nourishing the hope that if his *amour-propre* were piqued, he would outdo himself.

"You've succeeded in interesting me, Old Man. Note—and I don't wish to vex you—I was expecting that decision after your insistence on the Queen's change of attitude and your intuition of bad luck. I assume also that the telephone call had a determining influence on her conduct. I think it's time to tell me how this woman, just and sensitive as you have described her, could undergo so abrupt and unforeseen a change and make a decision so inhumane."

"This is what you are going to find out, Monsieur, as I myself did that very day.

"I was, then, at the home of the condemned's mother, and it was the Queen's secretary who telephoned to apprise me of the fatal verdict. I was too perturbed to repeat her message, but the mother immediately understood what it was by my wild look and the pallor of my face. As I have said, she was a woman of remarkable courage. She did not burst into vain tears; she had no word of recrimination. After a spasm she quickly controlled, she spoke in an authoritative tone:

" 'Ask her if this decision is irrevocable? If there is no longer any chance to save my son?'

"I transmitted her request, so upset that it's a miracle the secretary understood my whispering.

" 'Listen,' she replied, 'you know as well as I that the royal pardon represents the last resort of a man condemned to death. The sole remaining chance would be for the Queen to change her mind. That she can do up to the last moment, but I can't conceal the fact that this is a forlorn hope.'

" 'I am going to throw myself at her feet!' cried the mother when I had reported the secretary's words. 'She will listen to me!'

" 'I don't think that can shake her,' commented the secretary when I reported this. 'The Queen has not decided without mature reflection. If, like me, you were *au courant* with everything underlying this matter, you would think, as I do, that there is only one chance of salvation for the condemned, only one and, I repeat, very weak at that.'

"Aside from the quite natural feeling the secretary experienced at having to announce such sad news, I seemed to catch an implication I could not understand through her words, uttered in a reticent manner.

" 'I must see you alone,' she resumed after a silence, 'to put you in possession of the facts that have motivated this decision. Doubtless this is a betrayal of professional secrecy, but at least my conscience will not reproach me.'

"I arranged a meeting with her for that very evening, after having informed the mother of the faint hope the secretary had allowed me to glimpse, but I left her without being able to find words of comfort, promising to return the next day.

"The conversation I had with my friend the secretary tore the veil that had been blinding me, but at the same time it plunged me into a flood of unfamiliar feelings. When we were once again face to face, I reproached her bitterly for the words of hope she had given me before my audience with the Queen.

" 'They weren't given irresponsibly,' she protested. 'At that time the Queen was well disposed toward the condemned and ready to grant her pardon.'

" 'And what happened then?'

" 'There was the telephone call that interrupted your conversation. Do you remember?'

" 'How well I remember! I had an intuition of some fateful intervention.'

" 'That it was. It concerned her son. He is very sick.'

"Monsieur, I had thought as much. For a doctor to have been permitted to call the Queen directly, for the secretary to have decided to pass on the message to her, must have meant that the health of someone very dear to her was seriously endangered and required an urgent decision. The one human being to justify such precipitousness was her own son—the Queen's only son—concerning whom a rumor had been spreading in the kingdom that he was suffering from a grave illness, the exact nature of which was unknown. I had guessed as much without being able to imagine why this ailment threatened to influence the royal decision.

"That, Monsieur, is exactly what I learned from this woman of great intelligence bound to me by a very old friendship. The son, a young man of twenty, exactly my client's age, was suffering from a cardiac ailment, which, according to the doctors, would leave him little time to live. A single remedy, the one chance for survival: to borrow the heart of another, a healthy heart. . . . I see that you are beginning to penetrate the hidden reasons of the Queen's questions. What is involved is a rare example of maternal love. Brutally confronted with this sublime and cruel reaction of a mother, I was wonder-struck and indignant at the same time, as I imagine you are at this moment."

"Indignant first, Old Man," I murmured, "and wonderstruck next. But I suspect that by now your wonder has prevailed over your indignation."

He shook his head, replied only with a smile, and launched into digressions that quickly exasperated me.

"A heart graft, Monsieur, a cardiac transplant, in your jargon. Note that even at that period such techniques were not foreign to us. The Kingdom of Shandong does not scorn scientific research that seems worthwhile. Our surgeons—a great many of whom, I admit, have been schooled in your Western institutions—are able to carry out the most delicate operations, this one particularly, which was not yet performed in the West. The surgeons of the royal family had made grafts of this kind upon numbers of animals and upon two or three human beings, always with success.

"Unfortunately, adequate hearts available for such an operation are scarce among us even more than among you. Although we are in the vanguard of certain sciences and techniques as long as we regard them as beneficial to

26

the human race, we are retrograde in many other domains. We have not thought it advisable to develop our industry as you have. Herein we find advantages: The air has remained pure and salubrious on our snowy peaks. We have very few factories, few shipyards, no airplanes, a single railroad and, above all, almost no automobiles."

"I don't hold that against you, Old Man. But take up the thread of the story. All these details of your industrial development or, rather, lack of it, hardly excite me."

"Their connection with my story, however, should be evident, Monsieur. No automobiles, no car accidents. One railroad, very few railroad accidents. No factories, no shipyards, no industrial accidents. In a word, almost no accidents in the Kingdom of Shandong, a fact that ought to be considered, generally speaking, a godsend but that may turn out to be disastrous in particular cases, even tragic for the man of science in search of a young, sound heart to replace a defective organ. Can you understand the terrible dilemma of the surgeons responsible for the health and life of members of the royal family?"

"I understand, Old Man," I murmured, "I understand."

"Among us," he insisted, as if I had need of fuller explanation, "most of the people die of old age, with a heart worn out, entirely unfit for a transplant. . . . In this connection, can you see the reason the Queen displayed such interest in the health of the condemned young man, the reason she was at great pains to learn the possible presence of family weaknesses? After the secretary's revelations, the Queen's behavior immediately seemed obvious."

"I repeat that I do understand, Old Man. Just any heart at all is not good to replace one that is ailing, especially to make royal blood circulate."

"And there I had insisted on the excellent physical condition of my client, in a sense condemning him to the Queen's choice.

"Then, after a worse crisis, more alarming than the others, the practitioners had thought that a cardiac transplant could save the young prince only on condition that it be carried out within a few days. Since the chances of a suitable accident occurring in so short a time were extremely slim, almost nil, the Queen had made her decision at once and refused the pardon. My client was to be executed in two days, and all the arrangements had been made, so my friend the secretary informed me, for the surgeons to obtain the heart and conduct the operation under the best possible conditions."

The Old Man was silent, seemingly plunged in deep thought, his eyelids lowered. I, too, remained silent a long while.

"I thank you," I said at last. "Though morally ambiguous, your story is interesting on more than one point."

"Monsieur," he answered, opening his eyes, "it is not ended."

"As to the end, Old Man, I think I can easily guess, and it's useless to dwell on it. Your client, toward whom destiny was relentless, was executed. The transplant took place, thanks to the providential heart, and I suppose, from what you have told me of the cleverness of your surgeons, the operation was successful. The prince recovered his health, and the mother continued to reign with wisdom and humanity."

"The last points are accurate, but you err in one important detail. My client was not executed. At the last moment the Queen granted the pardon."

"You see me consoled, Old Man. It seems to me the moral gains thereby. I surmise: the mother goes to throw herself at the feet of the Queen, as she had already said she was going to do, and the heart of the sovereign is softened by the despair of the other mother."

"You have missed the conclusion completely, Monsieur. Her supplications would have been futile. The secretary had left no doubt about that. In her opinion and those of counsellors, the Queen could not reverse herself without losing esteem. In order for her to modify her decision with dignity, for her ultimately to grant the pardon, which she did at the last minute, it was necessary to uncover a new piece of evidence."

"A new piece of evidence?"

"Just so, Monsieur—in legal terms, a fact that presented itself on the very night before the execution—barely, barely in time, heaven be praised!"

My storyteller of nights saddened by the poverty of my own imagination seemed on the point of wrapping himself in one of those familiar silences fated to whet my curiosity. Now grown impatient, I gave him no pause.

"Out with it, Old Man. Confessions of the real criminal, perhaps? You led me to believe that a doubt hovered about your client's guilt."

"Not in the least. The new fact was that a heart other

than my client's was placed at the disposal of the surgeons, a heart unhoped for."

"Was it one of those accidents you've asserted to be very rare in the Kingdom of Shandong but which must, nonetheless, occur at times?"

"You almost guessed it, Monsieur. An accident, if one wishes to call it that, since for certain psychologists a murder always admits of an accidental side. Yet I think this murder must be considered a manifestation of Providence rather than an accident."

"A murder?"

"A murder without the shadow of a doubt—one of those bizarre coincidences—one that took place on the very night preceding the decreed execution, and in a somewhat isolated cottage near the dwelling in which my client lived with his mother. A young man was savagely attacked at knife point. He was, again heaven be praised, an athlete in fine shape, bursting with health and, even happier fortune, a single man without living parents. No family. And, coincidence even stranger, it was none other than my client's mother who called the police that night."

"Chance and truly extraordinary coincidences," I observed.

"In my eyes, Providence," murmured the Old Man gravely. "It is true that these fortuitous interventions that run counter to our customary course, the routine course of the Universe, are sometimes difficult to attribute to their real cause. But I ought to tell you that on the evening before this sinister day I thought I should inform the mother of the secretary's revelations and of the one chance, infinitesimal, that remained for us. You may be sure I did not decide to do this without painful hesitation, but my old friend had insisted I do so and I allowed myself to be persuaded. As I have let you anticipate, the women played no negligable part in this affair. The secretary, about whom I have spoken little, for, in short, she had only a secondary role, gave me, I believe, the best advice I could have received. She, too, was the mother of a family, a fact that undoubtedly put her in a position to understand better than you or I the feelings of the principal characters involved. Having convinced me it would be futile for the condemned man's mother to go to implore pardon for her son, she had counseled me with such vehemence that I recall her words:

" 'But you must acquaint her with the exact situation in order that she pray heaven with all a mother's fervor that it call forth this very night the sole new fact capable of saving her son.'

" 'You think so?'

" 'I am certain of it. The mother would never forgive you for having left her in ignorance.'

"That is what the secretary suggested I do, Monsieur, almost forced me to do, I should say, with an insistence that moved me. And, having had occasion to appreciate the clearness of her judgment, I obeyed.

"So, you can easily imagine that tearful mother spending a sleepless night in prayer, in passionate prayer, imploring heaven to designate a victim other than her son. It is not surprising she was the first person alarmed by a frightful shriek, as she said, and that she was also the first to rush to the scene of the crime, since the victim was her close neighbor.

"Neither is it strange that it was she who warned the police in an instantaneous reflex, understanding that heaven had heard her prayer."

The Old Man again paused while I repeated thoughtfully:

"Heaven had heard her prayer. . . . Haven't you anything else to add?"

"Some small details of no great importance. Another neighbor, awakened with a start by the victim's cry, hastily put on an overcoat and in turn rushed toward the cottage. He reached it at almost the same time as the police. He was greatly astonished, for, according to him, no more than a few minutes had elapsed between the cry and his intrusion. And one thing more: The doctor who accompanied the police was surprised to realize that the young man had breathed his last in spite of deep mortal wounds only an instant earlier. In fact, he died almost under the doctor's eyes, a fact that facilitated the transplant. Monsieur, everything happened as if . . ."

"I wish to complete your thought, Old Man. Everything happened as if the mother's telephone call had *preceded* and not followed the murder."

"That is exactly what I mean, Monsieur. But after having reflected on these details—quite curious, I admit— I believe I have found a valid explanation."

He leaned toward me, again staring with catlike eyes.

"It's very possible, if not probable, that the mother, in the state of exaltation in which she found herself after hours of passionate prayer, had had a premonition of the attempt about to be made, that she had viewed the scene in a dream while believing she was living it, and that she had then rushed to alert the police. Such phenomena of second sight are fairly common in the Kingdom of Shandong and they even occur at times in your Western states, especially among women."

"Especially among women," I repeated. "Is that your opinion?"

"That is my opinion, and we should consider the dream, too, as an act of Providence, for it allowed specialists to find a body still warm and to operate with the greatest chance of success. Doubtless one must see even there an example of maternal love carried to its paroxysm: a prayer so fervent, it obliged Providence to manifest itself. Monsieur, you can envision my joy when I learned of this miracle. You can guess, too, that I did not forget my friend the secretary, whose advice had been so precious, or neglect to make her a gift sumptuous as my modest resources would permit."

"She deserved it, Old Man," I murmured. "I approve."

"I have very little to add, Monsieur. Having been saved, my client saw his sentence of detention remitted after a few months. As to the murderer of the young athlete, he was never discovered. The inquest appeared to be very difficult because of the evident lack of a motive for the crime. It was quickly abandoned at the Queen's order, so they told me."

"And the young prince?"

"He recovered and lived for many years, thanks to his new heart. The operation had been a great success."

"I should guess," I said, in my turn looking into the

eyes of the Old Man, "I should guess that the organs of the victim were in good condition, in particular the essential organ."

He sustained my look and replied, emphasizing each and every word with quite solemn conviction:

"You guess rightly, Monsieur. One can trust in Providence. It leaves nothing to chance once it has decided to intervene. The criminal hand had guided the blade with special care. It had neatly cut the throat and had taken pains not to damage the heart."

# The
# Marvelous
# Palace

$M$ONSIEUR," began my raconteur of the night, "the story that comes to mind this evening implies a twofold moral. The first I might express in this way: When men of energy are stirred by creative passion, they always carry to a happy conclusion the task they've set themselves, no matter how arduous and difficult; they triumph over every obstacle and refuse to be discouraged by the criticism leveled against them."

"That hardly seems very original, Old Man."

"The second is, that once they've attained their ultimate aim, the work brought to a close by virtue of their intelligence, their labor, their desperate drive, is revealed to be useless and derisory because one little detail has escaped their genius."

"That aspect pleases me more. I, too, have noted a similar phenomenon quite often. Did you play a part in the adventurous undertaking that you are thinking of? I'll be delighted to hear about it."

"My part was episodic and unobtrusive; its promoters were the powerful ministers of the Kingdom of Shandong. In fact, it was a collective undertaking that couldn't have been carried out advantageously except with the collaboration of all the members of this élite."

"I'm always mistrustful of collective efforts," I said musingly. "I'm all ears just the same—if you've nothing better to offer me."

"A collective undertaking, to be sure, but the real promoter, the principal pioneer, was our Minister of Statistics."

"The Kingdom of Shandong had a Minister of Statistics?"

"He was actually the most important minister of all, Monsieur, the one who had fiscal charge and took precedence over his colleagues. At that period the minister was an eminent man with qualities recognized by everyone: he was highly intelligent, a prodigious worker, and had a pronounced liking for mathematics—he had graduated from one of our most outstanding schools, one that is not a whit inferior to yours and in which no branch of scientific instruction is neglected. He was a man of perfect equanimity and never got involved in anything without having studied the facts methodically. He knew better than anyone else how to interpret the statistics, all centralized in his ministry, seize their import, and draw conclusions useful to the administration of the kingdom.

Every day he himself spent several hours studying the masses of figures his underlings submitted.

"One day the statistics on criminality caught his attention, particularly those on first-degree murder, a crime subject to the death penalty and often punished in that way. I had the luck to be present, as it were, at the birth of the idea, for after he had pondered the matter, he summoned the Minister of the Interior, who happened to be one of my friends and who later told me of their meeting.

"My friend found his colleague bent over two sheets of a report, at his left a table of figures, at his right a graph, his face showing all the marks of an intense interest. He stopped in order to query the visitor the moment he entered:

" 'Have you seen these figures and the profile of this curve?'

" 'I have, Your Excellency.'

"I've told you, Monsieur, that the Minister of Statistics took precedence over all his colleagues, who always addressed him respectfully.

" 'Have you observed that the number of murders in our kingdom has tripled in recent years?'

" 'That hasn't escaped my notice, your Excellency.'

" 'Have you also observed that the rate accelerates with time? It's as plain as day from the curve of this graph that in ten years the Kingdom of Shandong will teem with murderers like fish in the sea.'

" 'Alas, I've observed the same thing, and, I find it highly alarming.'

" 'Alarming! alarming!' fumed the Minister of Statistics. 'We are not in the government to entertain qualitative judgments. We are here to take the requisite measures to avert danger. Do you have any interesting suggestions to make in this regard?'

"The Minister of the Interior, only recently appointed and still inexperienced, mentioned some of the commonplace measures that naturally come to mind in this kind of situation: expansion of the police; creation of special brigades; strengthening of repression. But he had the feeling his superior was listening with only one ear and was pursuing a very different train of thought. He was sure of it when the other interrupted him:

" 'Agreed. All that is good but not good enough. We took similar measures some years ago; now look at the result on that curve. Disappointing; the increase has scarcely been affected. One must not refuse to look. We should be prepared to face up to the prospect of thousands upon thousands of murderers in a few years, and then of thousands upon thousands of men condemned to death. The logical conclusion is that if we do not act now, we shall be guilty of not making provision for the construction of a suitable center for executing this army of assassins. Am I not right?'

"Such were the premises of this enterprise, Monsieur. The basic idea had been born. It made headway, as you'll see."

"I like that logic, Old Man," I said to encourage him. "Your Minister of Statistics seems to have been remarkably intelligent."

"Remarkably, Monsieur. But once the idea was born,

40

he realized—regretfully, I believe—that he couldn't put it into execution with the resources of his own ministry alone. The dimensions he was bent on giving this center, a breadth that had appeared to him in a sudden moment of exaltation, made necessary a collaboration with many other services and, first and foremost, an exchange of views with persons other than the Minister of the Interior, who did not seem to him entirely equal to the problem. After reflecting a few moments, he realized that the Minister of Land Resources was the most qualified man with whom to discuss the question. He immediately sent him a confidential message, asking him to come to talk with him about a decision of highest importance that could not be delayed. Lured by the solemn and mysterious tone of the message, the colleague came promptly. My friend, the Minister of the Interior, was invited to remain, three heads being better than one. As a result, I was still in a position to follow the early developments of the idea.

"No sooner had the Minister of Land Resources been told about the project than he was won over. He, too, had graduated from as highly regarded a school as the one his colleague had attended and in which administration and organization were cultivated as arts.

" 'If I've understood you correctly, Your Excellency, you want to centralize executions at a single point in the kingdom.'

" 'Precisely. Centralize and modernize.'

" 'You'll always find me on your side in such a policy. A center, then, that must have important dimensions.'

" 'Considerable. Look at the profile of that curve.'

"The ministers bent over the graph, poring intently over the alarming line.

" 'For the next three or four years a fairly limited area would suffice—about six acres,' ventured the Minister of the Interior timidly. 'And yet, if we are to look toward a more distant future . . .'

"That touched off an indignant protest from the Minister of Statistics, who called on his colleague of Land Resources to comment on this narrow viewpoint.

" 'Six acres! Listen to that! What do you think?'

"The minister appeared to give the question his careful thought and then calmly said:

" 'I think we ought not to let ourselves be caught napping—as, for instance, has happened in the field of national education, where the estimates of required new buildings have always been ridiculously below the needs.'

" 'Now you're talking! They would never forgive us for making the same small-minded errors as the Department of National Education. One never takes a sufficiently large view in affairs of this sort.'

"The Minister of the Interior, aware he hadn't been on top of the situation, managed to get himself out of the difficulty:

" 'If you will permit me a remark, Your Excellency, I suggest providing in the new center not only for the buildings of execution but for a model prison to which those condemned would be taken immediately after the verdict.'

" 'Bravo!' cried the Minister of Statistics. 'At last you've grasped the idea. That's just what I've been thinking. Centralize and modernize, by heaven! A prison that will have nothing in common with those hovels scattered throughout our land, with those antiquated and wretched dungeons that the Minister of the Penitentiary System was deploring in my presence only a few days ago. . . . Have someone go find the minister.'

"The Minister of the Penitentiary soon appeared. He had nothing but praise for a centralization that would considerably facilitate his task. After he had put forward a number of general ideas on his conception of a model prison for those condemned to death, it was plain the center would have to cover a considerable area. The question of the site to be acquired once more became acute.

" 'I think,' declared the Minister of Statistics authoritatively, 'that we should have at least a hundred acres. And, what's more, with possibilities of expansion.'

" 'A hundred acres,' murmured the Minister of Land Resources thoughtfully. 'I suppose I could find them in the remote countryside.'

" 'Out of the question. A model center of this sort ought to be in the capital, or at least in its immediate vicinity. Moreover, it will be a tourist attraction. Finally, one must consider the cost.'

" 'The cost, of course,' said the Minister of Finance, whom no one had heard come in.

"He hadn't been invited yet, Monsieur, but word had begun to spread throughout the government building that something big was under way in the Bureau of Statistics. He couldn't resist the temptation to sniff what was in the wind."

"That makes how many ministers in the office, Old Man? I'm beginning to lose count."

"Five, Monsieur, but that is only the start.

" 'The cost, quite so,' retorted the Minister of Statistics, without appearing surprised at his colleague's presence. 'It's a point I never lose sight of. Now, all the statistics show it's in the capital that the greatest number of criminals are to be found. It's in the capital that they are judged. The cost of displacement will thus be limited to a rock-bottom figure.'

"For the time being the Minister of Finance found nothing to fault in this logic and was content to listen in silence to the rest of the debate. The Minister of Land Resources was turning things over in his mind.

" 'There would be,' he said finally, 'the land for the Petite Ville. More than a hundred and fifty acres.'

" 'The Petite Ville?'

" 'The land is situated due north of the capital in the nearest suburb. There was some question of constructing a small town there; hence the name. But nothing has been decided yet.'

" 'I need that land!'

" 'It doesn't belong to the kingdom but to the capital. Therefore the capital's Council must decide on its allotment.'

" 'Someone call the Council! It can't refuse to grant the land and collaborate in a project that will greatly enhance the standing of the town.'

"But the hour was late and the members of the Council couldn't be convened that evening. The ministers, however, considered the land to be already acquired and began to talk among themselves to bring into focus the large outlines of an overall plan, indispensable before soliciting the King's approval. He was a young prince with plenty of drive, always favorably inclined to innovations and the Minister of Statistics usually managed to convince him, provided he had a coherent project.

"They worked the greater part of the night. Secretaries, hastily awakened, carried urgent messages to renowned architects. Others went from office to office looking in the files for this or that indispensable record. At dawn, as the sky over the capital grew light, the Minister of Statistics came to a halt, pencil poised in air.

" 'This plan begins to take shape,' he said; 'now it's for the specialists to work on. What remains for us to do, this very morning, is to find a name for our new center.'

"His colleagues agreed. They all began to search for a richly suggestive name, one worthy of the splendor the establishment was beginning to take on in their imaginations as well as in the considerable number of sketches feverishly drawn in the course of the night. Because they found nothing fitting, the Minister of Statistics didn't hesitate to have the Ministers of Propaganda and Fine Arts awakened, as their advice could be invaluable."

"I see, Old Man, that the collective work continues to develop its tentacles."

"Later on it did so even more, Monsieur, when the architects became involved as well as the Council of the capital, the research departments, the contractors, not to mention a legion of businessmen, middlemen, lawyers, judges, and even modest ministers of worship like me. But to return to that feverish dawn when it was still a limited committee—to be exact, seven ministers, the last to arrive being the ministers of Propaganda and Fine

Arts, still only half awake, yet very soon carried away by the enthusiasm of their colleagues and eager to add their stone to the construction of a monument that would be the glory of the realm of Shandong. For the moment it remained only to bestow a name. Center for Executions, advanced earlier by the Minister of the Interior, was rejected unanimously.

" 'The Palace of Executions,' suggested the Minister of Land Resources.

" '*Palace* doesn't strike the ear harshly,' admitted the Minister of Fine Arts, but *Executions*—frightful, unaesthetic. No.'

" 'The Palace of Higher Works?'

" 'That sounds like the jargon of the local law courts,' protested the Minister of Propaganda. 'You won't enlist the support of the masses with "Higher Works". I admit, nonetheless, that *Palace* is acceptable.'

"They discussed the matter at still greater length, Monsieur. Not one of the names proposed brought unanimity. Then the Minister of Propaganda said a few words:

" 'Exellency, gentlemen, and dear colleagues: sometimes we look for suggestive titles that are too sophisticated. We are wrong. Experience has taught me that it's often the simplest name that appeals to the crowd and holds its attention. The name of the Petite Ville is already familiar. It is simple and not readily forgotten. Why not *The Palace of the Petite Ville?*'

" 'A little dry,' objected the Minister of Fine Arts. 'There should be a descriptive word.'

"My friend, the Minister of the Interior, who later reported this discussion, affirmed that all at once the epithet *marvelous* burst spontaneously from the mouth of everyone present. The Marvelous Palace of the Petite Ville was christened, Monsieur."

"Simple in effect and easy to remember," I remarked. "And besides it makes an alexandrine."

"I believe I can guess what you mean, Monsieur. The Minister of Fine Arts was truly seduced by a certain poetic rhythm. A great forward step had just been taken. The baptism was celebrated that morning with a sparkling wine the Minister of Statistics had sent up."

"I should have supposed," I remarked, profiting from a pause, "that a Minister of Statistics would live barricaded behind his files. I shouldn't have imagined him a man of action."

"Usually he was not. It probably had required a special occasion. A special state of mind that day? The fact is that after a glance at a column of figures and a curve, an unaccustomed energy had transformed him. A sudden rush of excitement, which lasted just long enough for the accomplishment of his design. When a man given to abstract calculation is touched by the angel of creativity, Monsieur, one may expect great results. One must admire the fierce energy that made him surmount all the obstacles encountered because of the hugeness of his undertaking.

"He first had to convince the King. It wasn't very difficult, since the young prince was always inclined, as I've said, to approve a project tending to modernize his kingdom. Then there were criticisms, some violent, from gloomy souls who found his plans too grandiose for a state as limited in extent as the Kingdom of Shandong.

The word megalomania was even used. The minister succeeded in overcoming all barriers in the course of conferences, public gatherings, and, finally, in convincing most of the influential political figures that his project was not only reasonable but indispensable to the reputation of the state. During this time the architects were not idle —their exchange of ideas had brought forth a host of bold, original proposals, the best of which were kept. The structure of the palace was not slow to be put on paper and then materializing into three dimensions on the site formerly reserved for a small town.

"I'll pass over the work of the experts whom the Minister of Statistics had inspired and with whom he kept in daily contact in order to suggest, perfect, enlarge, and embellish so well that the completed palace deserved, beyond any doubt, the epithet marvelous that had been bestowed on it at its conception. If you want me to, I'd like to describe all this splendor just as it appeared to me when a small group of privileged persons, of whom I was one, was authorized to visit it a short time before its official inauguration."

"Do so, Old Man. I'm eager to admire this marvel."


"Then, Monsieur, I shall give you a general impression. What struck me at first was the unaccustomed grandeur of the different stops and the belt that linked them."

"A belt?"

"A belt that reminded me of your modern assembly-line factories. The general scheme had been conceived from the earliest projection at the request of the Minister for the Quality of Life in his concern to spare the condemned man all pain other than the supreme punishment. He was not to *walk on thorns,* to use an obsolete and barbarous phrase, but to be borne there effortlessly by a sort of moving tread. If you care to, let us follow that belt together, a belt that traversed the palace from the entrance to the exit.

"First, the prison. I won't describe it in detail, for it presents nothing particularly original. You should know simply that it had been conceived like most modern institutions of its kind, each inmate having at his disposal a room provided with every necessary comfort.

"The belt started from there and took the condemned to the first stop, the initial step of the fatal journey: *The Salon de Toilette.* This was by no means a mere corner for cutting hair and laundering shirts. It was a real salon, with baths, showers, massages, where one could have a complete toilette; where esthetic attentions were dispensed by specialists; and hair-dressing artists styled a suitable coiffure. The section reserved for women was especially elegant. Here they could choose their favorite perfumes and the garments in which they wished to die, with the sole restriction that the clothes present no inconvenience for the mode of punishment reserved for them.

"The belt picked up the condemned at the exit of the salon and brought them to the entrance of a building of imposing proportions, the largest, along with the cathedral, of those constituting the palace."

"The cathedral, Old Man?"

"We are coming to that, Monsieur. Let us run through the circuit in logical order. We have arrived before The Hall of Last Desires. So they had named the building after hesitating between *desires* and *wishes;* it alone covered an area of more than forty acres. Its realization had made for the close collaboration among all the ministers, particularly those of Fine Arts and of Leisure. Shall I explain its purpose?"

"The name seems explicit enough. More than forty acres!"

"The importance of this stop had seemed to justify such extensiveness. Set down at the entrance by the moving belt, the condemned were taken in charge by the hostesses of this paradisiacal place, where everything had been thought of to satisfy the ultimate desires of those who were about to die.

"Everything, Monsieur. We had lifted ourselves far above the last cigarette and the puerile glass of whisky customary in other countries. A restaurant occupied an important place in the hall. There the most exquisite, even the rarest, dishes could be prepared by an army of cooks chosen from the best of the realm and elsewhere. The wine cellar occupied a part of the basement and the chief sommelier prided himself on being able to serve wines and spirits that one no longer finds except on the tables of certain heads of state who are epicures. Nor do I have to tell you that pleasures of the flesh had not been neglected. A battalion of fantastic creatures, the most beautiful in the world, were kept at the disposal of the condemned, ready to respond to all their desires, the humblest, the maddest, the strangest.

"Everything, Monsieur, everything had been anticipated in this hall to ease the pain of death by changing it into an enchanting festival. Even drugs had not been left out. This hadn't been without some hesitancy on the part of the Minister of Public Health, who had found a pretext here to inject himself into the circuit in order to raise a solemn protest. But the Minister of Statistics, with his rigorous logic, had no trouble in demonstrating the futility of this opposition, his principal argument being that physicians themselves, those guardians of public health, currently prescribed morphine to calm the sufferings of the terminally ill and that health couldn't be impaired in any way by the absorption of drugs by unhappy men destined to die in the following hours."

"Hours? Am I to understand that the stay would last a long time?"

"It might actually be prolonged for some hours. The opportunity was especially provided for the satisfaction of man's noblest desires, answering to the highest aspirations of the human spirit, for which the hall was equally equipped. It possessed an extensive library both in the number and quality of volumes. There the works of the most famous poets and novelists stood side by side with those of ancient and modern philosophers who had left an imprint on their age. The condemned could read and reread certain texts of their choice, provided, of course, that the time for reading did not exceed a fixed limit. A concert hall, a cinema, a theater, a collection of recordings probably unparalleled in the world, also figured in this hall, as well as a museum in which the canvases of the greatest painters had been acquired at a huge price."

"To equip this section alone must have cost a pretty penny," I remarked.

"A fortune, Monsieur. But the Ministers of Fine Arts

and of Leisure, who had entered the lists, had succeeded in wresting the enormous credit necessary for it to surpass all the others in magnificence. In order to silence certain critics, they brandished under the noses of their detractors the well-known formula: *murder considered as a fine art,* declaring that it would have been scandalous not to apply it to lawful capital punishment as well as to common murder.

"Together their efforts had not been in vain. Monsieur, when I paid a visit there, The Hall of Last Desires impressed me as one of the artistic masterpieces of which the human soul can be proud. The material and spiritual perfection of a monument. I see it now as I did then and experience the deepest emotion."

My storyteller of the night paused, his face ecstatic with the brilliance of his recollections, while I tried with eyes closed to imagine the splendors he had described and to rise to the height of his enthusiasm. Soon he resumed in a steady voice:

"After spending an hour or more in The Hall of Last Desires however they desired, the condemned were brought back by the belt and set down in front of the next stop: the religious."

"It's here, I should guess, that you come on the scene."

"Humbly, Monsieur, as you'll see. But I must make a parenthetical remark to tell you about the discussions that took place in connection with the building of this station.

"From the outset a single chapel had been envisaged,

of which I was to be the only lay priest. As you know, in the Kingdom of Shandong the principal worship is the cult of Doubt, which necessitates few priests. I was then the only one in the capital. When I was asked my opinion on the religious stop, I asserted that there was no need for either an imposing edifice or decorative accessories. This cult, Monsieur, knows nothing of idols and scorns lighting effects. It is content with a muted atmosphere and soft light. The semi-obscurity is itself agreeable, a gray penumbra in whose bosom the spirit believes it distinguishes every now and then a feeble light, which flickers and, scarcely born, dies."

"Your religion of Doubt doesn't appear to be a very joyous one, Old Man."

"That is the way it is, Monsieur, and the élite among us are attached to it.

"To go on, a sober room, furnished with two armchairs —that's all I need to make the condemned man reflect on the uncertainty of his impending fate, while enunciating the elementary principles of the absence of faith, which is our essential credo."

"You've never before enunciated these principles to me."

"They are so evident that it seemed superfluous: In the matter of religion, every firm belief is presumption. No being is yet wise enough to be able to judge of the existence or nonexistence of a God or a cosmic consciousness. If one must, one can nourish the hope that the humanity of a few thousand years hence will arrive at a modest probability on this subject. But for the present, humility and wisdom consist in recognizing our inability and taking refuge in Doubt. That is Doubt's essential element, Monsieur."

"Simple indeed. I realize you would have needed only a tiny cell to develop these principles. But I have an inkling that your suggestion was not accepted by the ministers and that your project was adjudged too skimpy."

"Exactly. When I set forth my views to a committee, the Minister of Statistics objected:

" 'Simplicity? Certainly, for the cult of Doubt. Yet there are other cults.'

" 'Not widely accepted in our kingdom,' I replied.

" 'True. But should we count solely on the Kingdom of Shandong to support our palace? This unique monument is certainly going to attract foreign visitors, who will praise its beauty and efficacy throughout the world. It's reasonable to anticipate that a goodly number of states, more poorly equipped than we, will then be disposed to send us their condemned criminals. That seems to me more than likely. We should then be guilty of not being prepared to satisfy the demands of the numerous religions practiced in those states.'

"This observation, Monsieur, which tended to give an international scope to our monument, was received by the ministers with renewed enthusiasm. The committee decided on the spot that discreet contacts should be made with important political figures. The result of this inquiry was that several states were inclined to be relieved in this way of their own condemned prisoners, subject to a reasonable tariff. As for the Kingdom of Shandong, in addition to the prestige conferred upon it by this monopoly, it stood to gain in foreign credits, of which it had great need. It was then decided to construct a building capable of giving satisfaction to a large number of cults.

"So it was that The Universal Cathedral I've already mentioned was erected—it, too, a building of gigantic dimensions. In its interior different parallel bays were transformed into a Catholic church, several temples of your so-called reformed religion, a synagogue, a pagoda, a mosque, an orthodox church, and several other sacred edifices, each one constructed according to the practices of religious art relating to the particular kind of worship and with the architectural ornaments of the most sumptuous monuments of each faith."

"And your chapel of Doubt?"

"It hadn't been forgotten, but it seemed rather dull, crushed by the pinnacles, bell towers, minarets, and cupolas gleaming with gold and precious stones of the other religions.

"The belt was divided into as many links as there were religious bays, and the condemned man could hold communion consistent with his choice, purify his soul, repent, if he wished to, of his journey in The Hall of Last Desires, think of the delights close at hand in the garden of Allah, of his future reincarnation, or discuss with me the uncertainty of the Beyond.

"Past the cathedral there were several belts that took the prisoner to the stop considered by some the most important, the same principle having been applied there as had been applied in the multiplicity of churches. I mean that this stop was provided with diverse procedures of execution, almost as many as there are on this earth, so as to enable the condemned to depart this life in conformity with the mode dictated by the tradition of his country of origin. Shall I enumerate all the instruments, all the machines that the Minister of Statistics had succeeded in having installed at great expense in that stop called the Step of Liberation?"

"I beg you to do nothing of the sort, Old Man. I have confidence in the Excellencies of your country. I'm sure that not a single instrument, not a single machine had been overlooked."

"But what you should know is that there, too, each detail had been studied and the décor refined to dissipate the macabre atmosphere that generally pervades this last step. So it was, Monsieur, that the blades of the guillotine were cut of the finest diamond, that exotic and subtle perfumes annihilated the stench of the toxic gases, that the cords were of rich silk, and that the electrodes of the fatal bracelets were made of pure gold."

"Enough, Old Man. I now have, I believe, a quite clear vision of the Marvelous Palace. I assume that you've ended your description and that this Step of Liberation is the final one?"

"Not quite. I must still mention the Step of Recovering the By-Products. One last belt loaded the bodies and took them toward this stop. It was a sort of hospital. There, in successive pavilions, all the organs having any utility whatever for humans deficient in them were set aside by medical specialists. Eyes, kidneys, hearts, livers, blood, and many other precious substances were collected when they were found healthy and were expedited by the most rapid routes to the centers of utilization.

"That's what the Marvelous Palace of the Petite Ville was like, though my description, I'm afraid, may have given you only a feeble idea of its splendors. Spurred on by the ministers, an army of architects, entrepreneurs, technicians, artisans, artists, had given their best to realize a project without precedent. Monsieur, on this fabulous edifice were lavished more nights of work, more gray matter, more talent, more gold, too, than on any industrial complex. When I add that a gigantic cupola, sky blue, covered the whole of it and was visible from several surrounding areas, you will understand how moved, how enthusiastic we were—'we' meaning the few privileged who were admitted to visit it after the last links of the belts had been tightened, after the last coat of paint had given it its final luster—that is, about a month before the official inauguration."

"That inauguration, Old Man, should have given the occasion for quite a moving ceremony."

"Alas! Monsieur."

"Alas! Am I to understand it was spoiled by some unforeseen incident?"

"The ceremony did not take place. The belts never functioned. The stops remained unused. The cathedral bells never had any reason to chime. At the end of a few months the metals were covered with rust, grass began to grow between the links of the belts, while vagrants sometimes came to seek shelter in The Hall of Last Desires. After some years, alarmed at the enormous expense of the protection and maintenance these treasures required, the ministers decided to dismantle the palace, to auction the works of art as well as the materials that could be used in industry and in the construction of low-cost housing on the site of the Petite Ville. I've almost finished, Monsieur, yet you seem disappointed."

"A little, I confess. To be sure, your story presents some interesting aspects, but I'm afraid I can't make sense of them. To spend so much brain power, sweat, talent, and money, only to let buildings rust in disuse, is a venture that may seem admissible to the subjects of Shandong, but nobody in the West would put up with it. I shouldn't dare to relate this extravagant adventure. But there you are, I feel it, keeping one last revelation up the sleeve of your overcoat. In fact, you haven't given me the essential fact. Why did this fabulous artistic-industrial complex have such a pitiful fate?"

Now that he felt I was tortured by impatience, the spiteful old scoundrel extended his habitual pause interminably.

"Have you forgotten what I warned you of at the beginning of the story? Everything had been foreseen save one detail, one petty detail, a very understandable omission among so many accomplishments but a fatal omission for the future of our poor palace. The death penalty, the death penalty, Monsieur!"

"What about the death penalty? Speak up, Old Man!"

"It was abolished, Monsieur, not only in the states we counted on to make up the money but in the Kingdom of Shandong itself. Actually, for several years before, everyone had had an idea that such a measure would be taken. Our ministers, they alone, blinded by creative passion, had not accepted it. Our young prince, idealistic and full of liberal ideas as well as being a friend of progress, let himself be persuaded by a vast campaign in favor of the abolition and signed the decree only a few days before the date set for the inauguration of the Marvelous Palace of the Petite Ville."

# The
## Laws

*I* ENCOUNTERED my storyteller at a street corner after hunting for him a long time. A painfully limping imagination had almost paralyzed me for several months, and once more I was reduced to begging help of any muse at all, though she appear in the form of a centenarian with a cranium polished as ivory. I was in a morose humor and kept sardonically repeating to myself the heresy uttered by a philosopher of long ago: "One will end by realizing that there is no perfect subject for the novelist," while fulminating against the nonsense, the folly, the effrontery of such an assertion.

As soon as I caught sight of the Old Man, I took him by the arm, forcibly drew him into our habitual refuge,

63

and implored him to tell me a story. This time he had to be cajoled, for he, too, was in a sullen mood and at first did not respond to my urging except by mumbling—from which I had the feeling his present cares were beclouding his memory. However, after I had cunningly maneuvered the conversation, I knew by a certain reflection in the pupil of his eye that little by little his mind was freeing itself from the dark contemporary mist to soar toward the light of his past, a past rich in curious recollections. Then I pronounced the words: Southeast Asia. That brought him up sharp. He began his recital in the gruff manner he sometimes adopts, with a stern vehemence that sounded as if he were reproving an imaginary adversary.

"I should tell you, Monsieur, that the corps de ballet of the royal dancers of Shandong was made up of the most beautiful, the most graceful girls, not only of our country but even of all the Southeast Asia you have just mentioned."

"I have no doubt of it, Old Man."

He embarked on some general considerations that seemed out of keeping with the promising start of his story.

"That same Southeast Asia where, during the Second Great War, the Japanese converted the rubber of the conquered plantations into petroleum, whereas the Americans in the same period manufactured tons of rubber from the petroleum they possessed in abundance."

"One moment," I broke in. "Does this have any connection with the story I am waiting to hear?"

"No direct bearing, but a philosopher might discover

64

in it a distant relationship in the abstract realm of incongruity."

"I'm not a philosopher, Old Man. Get back, I beg you, to your royal dancers."

"For a girl to be admitted among them was an enviable honor," he resumed meekly, "since an accomplished dancer no longer had to be concerned about her future. The gifts she received more than sufficed for her livelihood, and when she reached the age of retirement, the King granted her a pension that made her safe from want. Moreover, those who solicited this place submitted to a very difficult examination that only those possessing both a flawless physique and a perfect knowledge of the dance could hope to pass successfully.

"Among this elite, Monsieur, the dancer Sinar shone like a glittering star with the triple brilliance of youth, beauty, and talent. I had often admired her in the course of performances the corps de ballet would give from time to time in the public plaza, for no law of our realm was opposed to a monk's contemplating the grace and perfection of form."

"Wise laws," I observed.

"Very wise. I'm happy you have taken note of this, for the events that follow put into sharp focus the excellence of these laws, while at the same time they indicate their importance in our lives. They had been dictated by a successsion of sovereigns as just as they were circumspect, who knew how to surround themselves with the most able experts."

"You were speaking of Sinar the dancer and of her marvelous seductiveness."

"It is with reason I've compared her to a radiant star. I can see scarcely any other way of conveying the impression she created in the audience when she came onstage and began to interpret the dances, sacred or profane. Adolescents grew pale when she lifted her arms toward the sky, old men sighed, and priests like me began to regret having renounced the world. At my age, after more than a quarter of a century, I relive once more the feeling she stirred in our hearts."

"Continue, Old Man," I said as I saw him about to sink into nostalgic meditation. "The beginning pleases me. It lets me hope that for once you're not going to draw me into some sinister adventure. I'd rather hear you speak of Sinar the dancer than of the wise laws of your kingdom."

"It will be a question of both, Monsieur. I should tell you, too, that this girl had been blessed by heaven with not only all the physical graces but also with a sensitive and virtuous nature. To be sure, in our kingdom the dancers were not restricted to an unduly austere life. Our laws, which I cannot praise enough, were comprehensive in this respect. Chastity was the rule, yet only in principle. In fact, most girls led a very free life. Many had a lover among the court guards, and no one took exception to this conduct so long as it didn't cause a scandal.

"Such wasn't the case, however, with Sinar. She was pure as a lily and kept herself so in spite of the solicitations of which she was the object. No man had ever loosened her sash. She had rejected the advances of the noblest, and the circlet of fine gold she wore on her ankle and the rare pearl that gleamed in her hair were not the price of any special favor but represented merely the tokens of love and gratitude of a host of humble admirers. For the people loved her still more for this exceptional virtue and gave proof of their love by an enthusiastic ovation at every one of her public appearances. It was a sight to warm the heart."

"And one I justly appreciate."

"Now, alas, I must bring up less pleasant scenes. This girl, this queen of the dance, this radiant star, I was to come very close to, I, a humble man of religion, when I returned from a journey in a neighboring country. I had left the Kingdom of Shandong a few months earlier when she was at the height of her splendor and glory, flattered, adored like a goddess. I found her tarnished, fallen, debased—to sum it all in one breath, shut up in a dark prison."

The Old Man watched me a moment in silence, no doubt to make sure of the effect of this surprise. I hastened to utter a polite exclamation. Satisfied, he went on.

"So it was, Monsieur. After my return I went to the local prison, where I exercised functions similar to those of your almoners. It was my custom to visit the unhappy, to bring them words of encouragement, to make them forget their miserable state. I spent long moments with those sentenced to death, if there were any, doing my best to lessen their anguish."

I see what you're coming to, you old rascal, I thought to myself. Again you're going to lead me into the inferno of punishments. Do all your memories revolve around these horrors, or rather do you take delight in choosing to evoke the most somber among them for me? But I took good care not to let him know of this impression and confined myself to asking two questions:

"I thought the death penalty had been abolished in the Kingdom of Shandong?"

"It had been reinstated later by our sovereign for a very small number of crimes. After the Marvelous Palace had been dismantled, the convicts were imprisoned in the earlier sordid cells."

"I'm curious to know, too, how a minister of the religion of Doubt can relieve the anguish of convicts under sentence of death."

"It's extremely simple, Monsieur: By exciting their curiosity as to the problematical character of a future life. Having succeeded in inspiring such curiosity, this would dissipate their fears. Is your own curiosity satisfied? May I continue my story?"

"I'm not sure I've really caught these nuances, without doubt Asiatic, but do go on. I'm listening."

"Well, then, there were very few condemned to the supreme punishment. There was precisely one on the day I took up my duties again; one, and at that, a woman. You've guessed rightly; it was Sinar the dancer."

"That pearl, that star, that angel who possessed every virtue!"

"She herself. I was as astonished as you and terribly distressed when I learned of this unimaginable downfall.

"The prison director, a respectable and conscientious functionary to whom I had gone just to pay a courtesy call, told me of her lamentable adventure. In a word,

Monsieur, Sinar had one day found herself pregnant. I use this expression advisedly, for throughout the trial she protested vehemently against the accusations of the public prosecutor and defended herself against the charge of having had a lover. In tears she declared that she had been violated in spite of her fierce resistance. But when she was pressed by questions and revealed the name of her alleged attacker, she simply met with incredulity from the members of the tribunal. For she named one of the noblest princes of Shandong, young, rich, handsome, who had only to stretch out his hand to pick the most seductive women of the kingdom. The accusation appeared ridiculous. He was, however, interrogated with all the formalities due his rank, and he swore indignantly that he was innocent of the crime. He recalled that in the past he had paid court to the dancer but had turned away from her long before when faced with her indifference and had forgotten her.

"The judges were convinced that Sinar had invented this tale in her desperate search for some extenuating circumstance capable of saving her head."

"But I don't understand this condemnation, or even the trial! Didn't you yourself tell me morals were quite liberal in your kingdom, tolerance was great, and dancers weren't kept to strict accounting for their lapses of conduct?"

"True, Monsieur. If you would allow me to tell my story without interrupting me, you would know by now that the object of this trial was quite other than what you imagine."

"Go ahead in your own way."

"Well, then, Sinar discovered she was pregnant. And though she did not on this account risk any judicial action, she quickly realized that the birth of the child would have disastrous consequences for her. The King closed his eyes to the private life of the dancers on condition that it be discreet, but the punishment for a scandal was the immediate and final dismissal of the guilty one from the corps de ballet. Sinar would have to renounce the dance forever. It was an appalling disgrace for a young girl like her. She saw herself leading a miserable existence, dying of hunger, exposed to the derision of her former companions, whose jealousy had been aroused by her supremacy.

"Put yourself in her place, Monsieur. She had never worked. She knew only dancing. It's not surprising she should have been terrified by the sinister future that opened up before her. Not astonishing either that this child should become the symbol of misfortune. During the nights that followed the discovery of her condition, she lived tormented by a constant nightmare in which the child took the form of a demon vomited from hell to accomplish her ruin. This state of mind was revealed in broad daylight when, in the course of the trial, she herself avowed the obsession, which didn't exactly win the sympathy of the judges. Quite the contrary.

"Her despair very quickly became so unbearable that she was soon ready for any insane act to escape the haunting thought of the monster she carried within her. After renouncing suicide because of lack of physical courage, she figured out the only way to her salvation and didn't hesitate to take it in spite of its repugnance: she decided to do away with the child.

"I'll spare you the sorry details that were revealed at the trial. A matron consented to perform the wretched service for her in exchange for Sinar's gold bracelet. Unfortunately, Sinar was denounced by one of her companions, who had noticed her state. After the initial inquiry the abortionist made a full confession, and when the dancer was arrested, she confessed the crime of which she was guilty."

"A sad story, but rather banal," I said, disappointed.

"Banal, yet with terrible consequences in the Kingdom of Shandong. It's now, Monsieur, that you will see the first effect of our laws, and before long you'll wonder how, by every expectation, what should have been a happy fate was oddly twisted to the point of making these laws hateful—in a way, even grotesque."

"I'm not sure I'll wonder at this, Old Man. But go on!"

"The laws of our kingdom, as I've said, were just and humane, but they became severe when they touched on a vital necessity. Moreover, the act the dancer had committed in a moment of desperation was one society had to punish without leniency in the Kingdom of Shandong, because of its troublesome declining birth rate. An act so harmful to the state necessitated a suitable sanction, and voluntary abortion was punished by death.

"You'll understand why the court showed the greatest skepticism when Sinar spoke of rape: it was the only circumstance that could have brought with it a lightening of the penalty. Because the denials of the implicated prince left no further room for doubt in the minds of the judges, the poor girl had been condemned to death. For a fortnight while awaiting punishment she had been imprisoned in the dark cell where I was to find her.

"This is the account the prison director gave me, the functionary whose merits I've praised. After he had finished, while I was expressing pity for the prisoner's fate and inquiring about her morale, the better to comfort her, his attitude seemed rather peculiar.

" 'You'll see for yourself,' he replied absently.

"Then he began to scrutinize me silently with an insistence that seemed extremely disagreeable. He asked me my age (I was close to seventy at that time) and shook his head, muttering some unintelligible words. Finally, after an abrupt gesture, he came up to me as though he had something very important to tell me and began:

" 'Above all, I must put you on guard . . .'

"He stopped short, shrugged his shoulders, and just repeated:

" 'After all, you'll see for yourself.'

"I was about to ask him for an explanation, but he made a sign that the conversation was over and I left him to begin my rounds. Before I was even aware of it, I went straight toward the building of the prisoners under sentence of death and had Sinar's cell opened to me.

"I don't know, Monsieur, whether you've had occasion to experience the melancholy a place of this kind emits: four bare walls surrounding a pallet placed on a cement platform, a rickety table, and an ugly wooden stool. I was sick at heart before this hideous interior, which contrasted so painfully with the delicacy of the prisoner. She seemed to have grown pale, emaciated, with drawn features, but even in this miserable hole she radiated beauty. The coarse garment she wore did not succeed in hiding the harmony of her body.

"I did my best to dissimulate my sadness. I greeted her respectfully and addressed some friendly words to her, as I was in the habit of doing with the other prisoners. She was seated on the stool, half slouched over the table, her head in her hands. She had scarcely stirred as I entered and didn't seem to notice my presence. I rambled on for a long time without getting a response, without her making a movement.

"When finally I fell silent, at a loss for words, she remained prostrate a moment longer. Then, as I was about to leave her, she suddenly changed her position and came to life. But this reaction, which I had hoped for, brought me no satisfaction; on the contrary, it disconcerted me cruelly.

"The pupils of her eyes suddenly gleamed, but with so strange a brilliance that it caused me unbearable discomfort. Her look sought mine with a sort of passion. I had the impression that all at once she had been seized by a disturbing thought she clutched at desperately, a thought that repelled me instinctively without my being able to guess why.

"Little by little her expression took on the disquieting fixity of madness. It paralyzed me and left me incapable of the slightest initiative to escape her. In this sort of hypnosis I saw her get up and come near me after a furtive glance toward the door. She moved slowly and her intention suddenly appeared with inescapable clarity.

"This girl was offering herself to me, Monsieur. Any man in my place would have judged the same. Even for a man of religion without much experience of the world it was impossible to be mistaken about the meaning of her attitude and look. She was offering herself to me, a priest, an old man. The very outrageousness of this behavior tempered my first indignation, which gradually gave way to a feeling of sharp curiosity, so much so that I observed every gesture minutely."

"That doesn't astonish me, Old Man," I murmured. "I've always thought you were a man to keep your powers of observation under any circumstances."

"There she was, now quite close to me, Monsieur, and every quivering movement of her body a provocation. Yet in offering herself, there was a pathetic nuance that made her almost touching and that prevented me from ascribing to her a trivial show of mischief. Imagine a child, to whom a prostitute had taught the shameful mimicry of her trade, forced to put her lessons to use with an awkwardness, yet with a feverish passion, as if a stake of supreme importance depended on her trick's success. I would have been a fool (Hadn't I been for an instant?) to attribute her conduct to desire. In the depths of her look, which haunted me, I could read the anguish of failing to secure her ends. That is what I deciphered on her face when, after recovering my self-control, I pushed her away and held her at arm's length."

"You gave proof of fine self-control, indeed. Oh, incorrigible analyst! I congratulate you."

"My refusal, it was clear, caused her bitter disappointment. Now terror made her lips tremble. Her eyes filled with tears.

" 'I beg of you, have pity,' she murmured in a scarcely audible voice.

"I could find no explanation for her actions and words except a sudden fit of madness. At that very moment, as I was foolishly stammering some words to calm her, the sound of footsteps in the corridor put an end to this scene. The guard was approaching, and he began to unlock the door with a great jangling of keys. Sinar drew back, and in spite of myself I was upset by the reproach I read in her eyes."

"Strange behavior, indeed. Are you sure this girl was such as you've described her?"

"She had always been a model of prudence and modesty. As for her conduct in prison, it will soon seem to you even more out of character. But I must tell you about the turnkey who now entered the cell, for he wasn't an individual to pass unnoticed.

"The jailer was new in the prison. I hadn't made out his features in the obscurity of the corridor when he had opened the cell, I was so absorbed in the dancer's fate. I had noticed only his short stature and limping walk. When he entered I observed him at leisure, the more closely in that I was trying to avoid Sinar's eyes. I couldn't repress a start of disgust at his appearance.

"This man, Monsieur, was a monster. Nothing in him

suggested the slightest humanity either in his general bearing or in the details of his physiognomy. With dwarf-ish legs ridiculously short, buckling under the weight of too heavy a torso, from the back he could have been taken for a gorilla dressed as a man. But that illusion was dissipated by the sight of his face, and any comparison of that sort would have been an insult to the ape. I shudder at the mere thought of conjuring up his unspeakable ugliness. Picture him afflicted with an enormous mouth, swollen lips drawn back in a constant, abominable rictus revealing unspeakable yellow teeth. Visualize, too, this muzzle surmounted by unnameable vestiges, in which the most careful observer would vainly have sought the form of a nose long since eaten away by some kind of leprosy."

"I almost see the creature," I said. "There is no need to take delight in enumerating all these hideous details."

"I only wished to underline the overpowering revulsion this man's appearance would necessarily inspire in any normal being. It made me sick, and my disgust grew when I realized he was carrying a tray with the prisoner's pittance. On him fell the care of watching over her. He it was who brought nourishment morning and evening, who fastened around her delicate ankles the links chaining her at night, who observed her as he pleased through the peephole, who escorted her during the quarter hour of the daily walk to which she was entitled, and who quite often kept her company in her cell, as is the rule for those condemned to die.

"The thought of this proximity between Sinar and that hideous animal was loathsome to me. I went straight to the director's office, determined to get him to give the prisoner a different Cerberus. The minute I opened my mouth he became surly. He replied somewhat dryly that Rimo—that was the jailer's name—performed his functions well. As I persisted in my plea, he added that there was no need to be shapely in order to carry out these duties and that, on the contrary, the disgust Rimo inspired was an advantage in the eyes of the penitentiary administration.

"I left him, incensed by his words, and went to visit prisoners in other quarters. But the phrases I spoke to them that day had little meaning. I couldn't forget either the dancer's conduct or the jailer's appearance. I cut short my rounds and was getting ready to leave this sorry establishment when, passing near the sinister building of death row, I had second thoughts and went in again, moved by an indefinable curiosity. Only one of the cells opening on the corridor was occupied—Sinar's. I saw that the door was ajar, proof that the guard was still there.

"Why did my heart contract at this sight and why did the feeling that took possession of me resemble indignation? There were scores of harmless reasons to explain his presence. It was the hour for the end of the meal and doubtless the guard had gone to pick up the tray. Besides, wasn't it his duty to watch over the luckless prisoner at every moment and at times to keep her company, however painful that society might be for her? Nonetheless, in spite of myself, I slowed my step and approached on tiptoe.

"Rimo, in fact, *had* gone to pick up the tray. He had already done so and was getting ready to withdraw. I felt relieved and was about to make my presence known when I surprised a look on the dancer's face. Well, I was taken aback and my heart began to beat crazily. What I beheld lasted no more than two or three seconds. Then she saw me and the expression of her face that had affected me so much immediately disappeared, so completely that I could almost believe it was an illusion on my part. But I had received such a brutal shock that I felt unable to bear the presence of these two creatures any longer. I stammered some meaningless words and fled."

The Old Man paused and then stopped. I knew him well enough to see that he was trying to whet my curiosity and that I'd gain nothing by showing my impatience, harrying him with questions. I merely remarked nonchalantly:

"Such an emotion for you, Old Man! It must have been a very odd sight."

"Judge for yourself. I went home prey to a fever that tormented me all night, trying to persuade myself I had been the victim of a hallucination. It was senseless on my part to interpret a simple look as I was. For it was just that, Monsieur, which had upset me, Sinar's look, the same, exactly the same, as she had directed at me an hour earlier and in which I had read the same intention.

"Hadn't there really been that light in the pupils? Had I seen her, yes or no, make a move toward the hateful creature who was clearing her table, going through the same provocative gestures? At the time the meaning of her attitude had appeared obvious to me. Afterward I began to doubt the evidence of my own senses, and in the

course of the night I wore myself out trying to recon-
struct the scene, to be precise about every nuance. But
with each new attempt the image became more and more
clouded.

"I was finally convinced that I'd been dreaming, that
I was in process of constructing an ignominious world on
an optical illusion. Wasn't I even mistaken about Sinar's
gesture toward me? She simply needed a little pity; that
would sufficiently explain the imploring looks she turned
upon every being who came near her. I decided to go
back to see her the next day, hoping that closer observation would dispel my phantasm.

"Like you, Old Man, I hope so too," I said. "I hope
with all my heart you found it a mistake and deplored
it."

"You will be the judge, Monsieur. I went to the prison
early. Since I was known to all the personnel and could
move about at will, I gained entrance to the building
of those condemned to death. The guard was not to be
found in the room reserved for him. I was still upset and
made my way alone down the corridor, already oppressed
by a dim presentiment.

"I had guessed it. He was there again. The cell door
was closed, but I saw his bunch of keys with one in the
lock. Cursing my curiosity, but without even trying to
justify it in my own eyes by my duties, I approached
noiselessly and glued my eye to the peephole.

"The tableau I saw was to remain engraved in my
mind. Believe me, Monsieur—you who, I'm aware, some-

times tax me with cynicism—I experienced such disgust
that I felt my face flush and my body begin to tremble
violently.

"She was offering herself to him, Monsieur. She was
offering her body to this monster. This time I couldn't
entertain the slightest doubt of her intention. This young
girl, who had rejected the advances of the noblest and
the most handsome *grands seigneurs* of the kingdom, who,
even if one didn't credit the excuse she gave for her
mishap, was guilty of just one moment of weakness, I
saw before me playing a game of infamy with an eye to
conquering a creature whose very touch would have
seemed an offense to the vilest of prostitutes.

"That is what I saw, Monsieur. She had come very close
to him. She had put her delicate, white fingers on his
enormous, deformed hands and was caressing them feverishly, studying him with the look that had so shaken me.
In spite of my indignation, I still registered all the details
of the scene and, paradoxically, the jailer's attitude soon
inspired a fury as great as did the dancer's. The face of
this brute expressed utter incomprehension and stupidity.
When she pressed her body against his (that's just what
she did!), he gave an inhuman snort of laughter and
pushed her away. I haven't invented a single fact: it was
he who pushed her away as if she were a pest!

"But she refused to give up. Humiliated, she shame-
lessly returned to the charge; her mouth was distorted in
a pathetic ghost of a smile, and she was murmuring words
I guessed at rather than understood—the very words she
had spoken to me: 'Have pity, I beg of you!' She implored
him, him too. Her behavior seemed dictated by an im-

perious necessity; it alone undoubtedly was enough to make her overcome her disgust. I felt it a bitter solace to observe this visible repugnance. Yes, she touched his hands again, those deformed paws, but the stiffness of her gesture betrayed a prodigious effort of will. When the contact occurred again, she jumped as if from an electric shock. I thought for a moment she was going to leap back, but she did nothing of the sort. Her hands still gripped the guard's and began to clasp them convulsively. I felt her to be close to the breaking point and measured the effort she made to bring her visage near this face with the foul lips and leprous nose. And again he was the one who pushed her away, this time so brutally that she fell on the concrete.

"If you think, Monsieur, she was discouraged, it's because you haven't yet understood the necessity that drove her or estimtaed the power of the infernal idea that had taken possession of her. I myself still hadn't guessed, crazed as I was, cursing her while trembling with horror at the baseness I had witnessed. She had halfway straightened up. She was dragging herself toward him on her knees. She clasped his twisted legs in her arms. She squeezed them, and her convulsive hands climbed the length of his monstrous body. With a violent gesture she tore off the fastening of her dress and offered her uncovered breast. . . . Offered! I say to you that it was a desperate prayer."

My old man, reliving the scene, was growing agitated. His indignant accents made his voice tremble. He saw I was watching him insistently and changed his manner.

"Above all, Monsieur, don't believe there was the slightest trace of spite after the advances she had made to me. The fury that set my body afire didn't originate in anything resembling jealousy. I've told you: I was already an old man, and my monastic life sheltered me from temptations of the flesh. I was revolted by the closeness of this girl and this being with nothing human about him."

"I suspected it only for seconds, Old Man," I said. "In your place, any man would have felt the same loathing. Then what happened?"

"I could keep calm no longer. I rushed into the cell with my arm raised, ready to strike her.

"She didn't move. Her face expressed no shame but betrayed only a frightful disappointment. He—the guard —didn't appear either surprised or embarrassed by my intervention. Again he gave a snort of laughter that seemed to be his sole mode of expression, shrugged his shoulders, and withdrew, pulling the door shut behind him.

"We both remained in the same position, I, with my fist raised, beside myself; she, on her knees, half naked, without seeming aware of it. Her look now expressed a melancholy so deep that my arm fell inert while a wave of compassion began to sweep away my anger. I struggled against this weakness, but I wasn't able to vent all my indignation except by avoiding her glance.

"I reproached her cruelly. I insulted her. I called her the vilest names. She seemed unheeding, appearing neither to understand my insults nor even hear them. When I grabbed her by the shoulders to force her to pay attention, she trembled and finally spoke, but I felt my heart freeze at the despair her voice revealed.

" 'Don't you see,' she screamed, 'don't you see at all that it's my only chance of salvation!'

"I remained a moment without stirring, struck by the intensity of this cry. And then, all of a sudden, the truth came to me.

"She was not acting out of wickedness, Monsieur, even less out of madness. Oh, no, she was not mad. Quite the contrary. An imperious reason was dictating every gesture. I was angry with myself for not having guessed it sooner."

"An imperious reason?"

"Imposed by an instinct, the most powerful of all, the instinct of self-preservation, you would say; the one that impels us to seize a red-hot iron with bare hands if it's the only means of saving ourselves from drowning. And the comparison is all too feeble, for what she had conceived in order to escape her destiny must have been a far more atrocious burn for her."

"I can guess, Old Man, but please be a little more explicit."

"Our laws, Monsieur. Again, our laws! The fatal logic of our laws imposed this self-degradation."

"You've told me they bore the stamp of humaneness."

"Both wise and just, far-sighted and temperate. Here is one, more reasonable than all the others. It had been inspired on the part of our kings by intentions at once humane and utilitarian—in other words, it had to satisfy both heart and mind, the two sacred poles of our feelings, our thoughts, and our acts. This law is not peculiar to the

Kingdom of Shandong but exists, I believe, in a good many countries. It stipulates: A pregnant woman cannot be put to death."

"I understand."

"I myself understood at that instant in which, shattered by her cry of distress, prey to an emotion that heightened all my faculties, I felt constrained to discover a reason for this unlikely conduct under pain of going mad. And, having found it, I experienced an immense relief.

"That was it, the logical explanation, Monsieur. A woman who is carrying a human life is sacred in the eyes of our law, as she is under your law. No civilized being would commit the offense and injustice of doing away with an innocent at the same time as the guilty. Her only chance of salvation was just that, a stay of execution at least, a postponement of a few months. Indeed, for the unfortunate person whose days are numbered, don't a few months represent eternity?

"She knew this law. No doubt she had learned of it before her sentence from conversations with the others in detention. The prison director affirmed later that her case wasn't exceptional. The text was imprinted on her brain. It buzzed in her ears night and day without giving her mind an instant's respite, and her implicit need made her live in a permanent obsession. She wanted to live, Monsieur. This desire drove out every other feeling, every other instinct, and was translated into a fierce will: to have a child."

My storyteller remained as overexcited as ever, but little by little his agitation seemed to change in nature. He began to manifest the amazement the lover of the bizarre experiences when he's confronted with events beyond his expectations. He appeared to deplore my lack of enthusiasm, and I read the reproach in his eyes.

"Don't you wonder, Monsieur, as I did, at the strangeness of this destiny? Its unique character dazed me. But at the same time I was still taken aback by Sinar, fascinated by this revelation, as I am to this hour."

"That sounds more like you!" I murmured. "I *do* wonder at her fate, Old Man. Oh! I do. Have no doubt of it. But I myself am not a centenarian and don't possess the resources of the religion of Doubt. That's why my rationalistic admiration is tinged with a little melancholy pity. Go on."

But as if he feared that a single one of the beauties he was revealing in this adventure might escape me, he racked his brains to release for me the perfume that intoxicated him.

"A child, a being whose very shadow she had detested and cursed to the point of taking its life—a child had been the cause of her ruin. Today, a child looked like the supreme chance to save herself. She had to have a child, no matter what child, and for that, a man, no matter what man. But few men entered the cell of a woman condemned to death. Our laws are rather consistent on this point. Do you see her there, casting a frantic glance around her, spying out—with what care, what anguish, what frenzy—the rare specimens of the male sex whom the law authorized to come near her? Do you imagine her, as I do, exerting every effort to display all her graces, all her charms, in order to win from one of them the saving gesture?"

"I see her, yet without being able to experience the exaltation this image seems to induce in you."

"She had tried it—I learned this later—with the prison director. But this austere functionary had too lofty an idea of his duty to let himself be tempted. On the contrary, he had taken measures to prevent her from attaining her ends. He purposely had assigned Rimo to her service, thinking that he, at least, would be safe from her attempts."

"Mistaken calculation."

"Just so. Little by little she had seen the field of possibilities narrow. Her lawyer had ceased his visits. The director never entered her cell alone. The prison doctor was an ailing old man. I had been her next-to-the-last hope. After me there was no one left but the monster. Only the monster could give her a child, Monsieur. The walls of her cell could not, nor could the hair pillow she saturated with her tears at night while ceaselessly working out diabolical maneuvers to capture a man. If a man with the plague had appeared at her door, she would have offered herself to his caresses. No one, I tell you, could be more loathsome than Rimo, yet she begged his favors. That is matter for a sage to meditate."

"I meditate as it suits the occasion, Old Man. But what was your attitude when you saw through her stratagem?"

"For a long while I was perplexed. The insults I had heaped on her were patently unjust. Her reasoning was logically irreproachable."

"I've always thought you were inclined to forgive many a fault in the name of logic."

"She had discovered a possibility to save herself. In

the name of principles that appeared more and more un-
certain to me, was I going to plunge her into the agony
of absolute despair during the few weeks remaining to
her? I didn't have the heart for it."

"Then you have a heart?"

"The right, if you prefer. I left the cell. I didn't reveal
the secret I had discovered to anyone. Later on, I kept
away from the building of the condemned prisoners. I
tried to efface Sinar and her jailer from my memory."

My nocturnal storyteller was silent a long while, pretending he'd ended his recital. But I knew him too well
to believe he could dissociate himself from the conclusion
of an adventure offering such curious elements.

"I take it you didn't see the dancer again," I said, "yet
her fate can't have left you indifferent."

"I saw her once more, Monsieur," he resumed, lowering his voice, "more than three months after this scene,
when the execution was to have taken place a few days
later. The prison director sent for me to take me to her.
He informed me that Sinar was very ill, that the doctor
couldn't do any more for her, and that only the presence
of a man of religion might be of some help to her. I
hastened to follow him toward the prison infirmary where
they had taken her. He gave me some hurried explanations on the way:

" 'She didn't withstand the shock she received from the
announcement of her pardon.'

"I stopped, stupefied.

" 'Her pardon?'

" 'Yes. I myself went to give her the news. The prince,

whom she had accused during the trial, had died a few days before, stricken by a sudden illness. Before his death he was anxious to ease his conscience and made a full confession of his crime. Sinar had told the truth: she had only yielded to violence. The people, who had always had faith in their idol, began to stir. The King hastily called his Council together, and pardoned the dancer. I didn't take any special precaution in announcing such happy news to her. However, I knew her to be ailing. The day before she had asked to see the doctor.'

" 'She had asked to see the doctor?'

"This time it was he who stopped to scrutinize me with a suspicious air.

" 'Didn't you have an idea of her condition?'

" 'I haven't paid her a visit in more than three months.'

" 'She was pregnant,' he growled.

"I uttered an exclamation. He ceased to observe me, shrugged his shoulders, and resumed his stride, and at the same time the thread of his story.

" 'When I informed her that she had been pardoned, she suddenly grew very pale. She was speechless, as though she didn't understand. I repeated my announcement. Then she staggered. Her face was convulsed as if from the effect of a violent pain, and she brought both hands to her belly before collapsing. The doctor arrived at that moment. He verified at the same time her pregnancy and a fatal accident.'

"We had reached the infirmary. My companion stopped again before opening the door.

" 'It isn't you, is it?'

"The furious glance I turned on him convinced him better than my protestations.

" 'Forgive me. For a moment I thought possibly . . . oh! out of pure charity. But I believe you. Then?'

" 'Rimo,' I murmured.

"He confirmed this with a sober air and again spoke hesitantly, as if he were looking for excuses.

" 'I couldn't foresee this. Nobody could possibly have imagined . . .'

"I cut him short angrily.

" 'She would have given herself to the Devil. That's what you ought to have imagined.'

"He lowered his head and we entered the infirmary. Sinar was dying. Her body was swathed in linens. The doctor, frowning, was washing his hands in a basin. I drew near her. Her dilated eyes seemed to comtemplate a vision of horror, but the features of her delicate face, strangely twisted, suggested incongruously that she was struggling against an insane desire to laugh. Her lips moved in a spasmodic trembling. I bent over her to catch her last words and at first couldn't hear anything except a sort of rattle resembling a laugh. Finally I made out one word, just one, but she kept repeating it at intervals in an accent of rage that distorted her voice: 'Useless, useless, useless.'

"Her gaze was fixed on a point behind me. Her eyes again grew big, and an appalling shudder went through her body. I turned my head and saw the guard Rimo. He had helped carry the unfortunate girl and stayed there in a corner, awaiting orders no one thought to give him.

I threw myself upon him and violently pushed him outside. When I came back toward the bed, Sinar was dead.

"The doctor wiped his hands and closed her eyes. The director approached him and spoke in a whisper. Then he came toward me and tapped me on the shoulder to arouse me from the trance in which I was lost.

" 'It will serve no purpose to noise this story about. The doctor is agreed. As for the guilty one, he will not boast of his heinous crime. Sinar died of a heart attack brought on by the emotion of her pardon.'

"I shrugged my shoulders. Emotion? Of course, why not? I myself knew well what sort of emotion had carried her off. From the moment when her mind was no longer hypnotized by the great excuse of necessity, the memory of her act had appeared to her impossible to endure. She had been able to bear the horror of it, but not the absurdity. And observe, too, Monsieur, the ultimate strangeness, which no doubt provoked the painful laugh of her last moments. To defeat her, Destiny had once more made use of the child, this phantom she had summoned with all her might after having once before put an equally fierce ardor into exorcising it. The knowledge of this queer coincidence plunged me into such confusion that, under the eyes of the scandalized functionary and doctor, I myself could not suppress an outburst of bitter laughter."

# The
# Limits of
# Endurance

$M$ONSIEUR, the story that comes to mind today, though it does present a few curious aspects, isn't exactly cheerful and does not exalt the virtues of mankind. I venture to put you on notice, since I've observed you sometimes seem reluctant to hear this sort of narrative. If you're in such a mood this evening, it would probably be better to give up our little talk and wait for a few days or weeks or even months until happier anecdotes come to mind."

"Blackhearted man!" I murmured *sotto voce*. "You have sensed that this is one of those evenings when I would sell my soul to Satan for an anecdote offering anything original. What's more, you are taking advantage of this to inflict on me another of your abominable concoctions." But aloud I went on, "Please, a story from you is enormously valuable to me, whatever its horror. Don't take advantage of my plight to toy with me like a cat with a mouse. Don't abuse your power. Spin your yarn, Old Man."

My centenarian deigned to smile and began thus:

"I must start, Monsieur, with the description of an illfated creature—a woman in her sixties, I believe, when I made her acquaintance, though she seemed much older. For a long time she had been suffering from a rather rare disease and was considered incurable by the specialists. Her husband, a baron of the region, without being very rich lived in comfortable circumstances and had spared no expense to have her cared for with all the resources of science. The three finest physicians of the realm took turns at her bedside, without, alas, succeeding in curing her and without even being able to alleviate her suffering, which was becoming more and more agonizing as her condition grew worse. The Baroness, Monsieur, endured a ceaseless martyrdom day and night; and that, in silence."

"In silence? A resignation, most assuredly deserving of admiration! a mind strongly tempered, a nature of exceptional courage, if her suffering was so great."

"Nothing of the sort, Monsieur. The Baroness was not resigned, at least not to pain, as you'll see. Her silence wasn't inspired by her strength of mind. The cause of it lay quite simply in the fact that she was mute."

"Mute?"

"Pathologically mute; afflicted with mutism, if you prefer. Deaf as well, and paralyzed in her lower limbs, and that for some years, from the onset of the mysterious illness that had struck her. A creature truly deprived, and deserving of the pity her case inspired in her immediate family. The unceasing, unbearable pain she endured had, of necessity, to be endured in silence. It could not be vented either in plaints or sobs or cries, but was reduced to being expressed in movements of the fingers, the drawing in space of the signs of the deaf-mute alphabet, which an instructor had taught her when her mind was still alert, though her body was already ravaged.

"This was how she appeared to me, Monsieur, when, at her husband's request, I paid her a visit. He set store by the presence of a priest as well as of doctors at his wife's side. And I had been chosen as replacement for a suddenly deceased bonze who had performed this duty before me. A piteous spectacle that affected me deeply: a body crumpled under the bedclothes, a face convulsed by pain, in which the paralyzed mouth was contracted without being able to utter a sound, not even a moan. The hands alone moved ceaselessly, making signs that nobody apart from her instructor could begin to understand. It was a sight so painful that the Baron had to turn his eyes away whenever he came near her bed. An old female servant, the only domestic of the château, who took care of her, did the same. And I, too, had adopted this habit, so depressing was the spectacle of those hands in perpetual agonizing movement.

"If, out of charity, I remained awhile facing her, after a few sittings of this kind I even pretended eye trouble and put on big dark glasses to disguise the fact that I was keeping my eyes closed. In that way, with the vision effaced, the silence prevailing in the patient's sickroom allowed me to forget the horror of her suffering."

"As well as her presence, perhaps," I murmured treacherously.

"Sometimes her presence, too, which no longer manifested itself to any of our senses. It is certain the calvary of this wretched woman in no way troubled the atmosphere of the château in which she lay dying. The Baron led a peaceful and ordered life. He was a simple man, devoid of passion. His leisure hours he divided between reading and the care of his garden. He had a library tastefully furnished and provided with a large number of rare books, where he spent every evening with delight. And he was very proud of his splendid garden, in which he had brought together unusual and magnificent flowers. Once a week a peasant of the vicinity came to do the heavy chores, but the squire himself saw to the current upkeep, devoting several hours a day to it."

"Old Man," I insisted, "if I really get an inkling of the atmosphere of this château, the Baroness felt herself completely isolated in her unhappiness."

"No, Monsieur, for almost every day, very often at the same time as my visit, she received the instructor, the one who had taught her how to express herself with her hands and who was the only one who understood her language. He served me as interpreter, translating into signs the consolation I unstintingly tried to give the poor woman."

"And for her sake, too, for this miserable woman, did you sing the virtues of the religion of Doubt? I recall from what you've stated before that its main object was to arouse curiosity by the prospect of an enigma. That seems to me a little cold, to give courage to a dying person suffering martyrdom."

"My religion, Monsieur," replied the Old Man in an offended tone, "possesses many developments of which you're unaware, many facets for distracting and comforting the unhappy, making them forget their woes. I always tried to present them in the most attractive form possible, particularly in the case of this poor woman. If parenthetical remarks of this sort don't put you off, I could tell you about the wager of Lac-Sap."

"Your parentheses, Old Man, are as precious to me as your recital of events. Who was this Lac-Sap?"

"A celebrated theologian as well as a remarkable logician who lived in the realm of Shandong a few centuries ago and whom I venerate, since he was one of the pillars of the religion of Doubt, if not its true founder.

"Lac-Sap, then, was the first to enunciate a very simple axiom that appears today with blinding clarity but that, before him, had escaped the subtlest minds, perhaps because of its extreme simplicity."

"What axiom?"

"This one: In matters of religion, the fact of believing or not believing is of absolute insignificance. It depends on a purely intellectual orientation, has no relation to notions of good and evil, is irrelevant to the idea of sin, and consequently cannot under any circumstances influence the eternal future of a being—his salvation, as you Christians would say. No sooner had it been enunciated than this axiom, indemonstrable and self-evident like propositions of its kind, was admitted as such by the entire population of the kingdom."

"Then?"

"Then Lac-Sap introduced the suggestion of a wager that captivated the populace and remained celebrated among us. The choice is between the existence or nonexistence of God and an everlasting life for the soul. Lac-Sap easily demonstrated that our interest lay in wagering on the latter eventuality."

"It's a conclusion that intrigues me, Old Man, but I don't quite follow the reasoning."

"It's clear nonetheless: In the event God does not exist, the wager would have scarcely any importance and, in every instance, you would have won it. In the opposite case, you would meet with a joyous surprise and experience the ineffable rapture that unhoped-for happiness brings—a joy that would not be felt anyhow by those who had wagered on an everlasting life, since they would be expecting it."

"Old Man, Lac-Sap's logic fills me with wonderment. I promise to meditate at leisure on its implications and deeper meaning. But do go on with your account if you've ended your parenthesis. Is it with such as this that you tried to make the Baroness forget her sad fate?"

"This and a handful of others."

"And what did she reply—or rather, have her interpreter reply?"

"She never answered, Monsieur. No doubt her suffering prevented her from becoming interested in my remarks. What the interpreter translated had no bearing on them. The answers were always the same: 'I am suffering martyrdom. I can't stand any more. I beg of you, help me to die. Tell the doctors to put an end to this torture. Dying, I shall bless them.'

"That, Monsieur, is what she expressed by means of her fleshless fingers convulsively molding shapes in space, her palms bathed in sweat. That is what the interpreter repeated to me at every sitting, shaking his head sorrowfully: 'Put an end to my suffering. Endurance has limits.' I hear her still."

"A case of euthanasia desired by the sick person," I murmured. "Were these remarks repeated to the husband?"

"To the husband and to the doctors. Because her prayer was becoming more and more insistent, more and more anguished as her condition grew worse, and since it seemed to me eminently reasonable, I took it upon myself to bring about a meeting, a sort of consultation, among the persons who came near her every day, for the purpose of discussing that eventuality. There were the three doctors who, as I've told you, were considered among the wisest, as well as the most conscientious, of the kingdom; the Baron, of course; the old servant who had been with her master and mistress for years and was almost a part of the family; and I myself.

"The Baron, who had granted my request rather ungraciously, I thought, asked me to spell out more precisely the meaning of this meeting. I repeated the desperate prayer his wife had made to me for the hundredth time. He kept his composure and asked me my opinion in a not-too-pleasant tone of voice. I gave it without beating around the bush. My religion saw nothing sinful in satisfying the poor woman's request. In my eyes, if her sickness was incurable and would lead to a fatal outcome very soon, as the doctors had let it be understood, it undoubtedly would be an act of charity to cut short her suffering. Wouldn't you have been of my opinion, Monsieur?"

"No doubt, as you said, Old Man, no doubt."

"Yet I was the only one to uphold this opinion, which was received in reproving silence. I remember the meeting very well and the setting in which it took place. The room in which it took place opened onto the garden, the beauty of which I've praised, and the only sounds reaching us were the joyous chirpings of its birds. No one could have imagined that a creature in a neighboring room was enduring the tortures of hell.

"After a long silence, the Baron began to speak, to ask each of the doctors, one by one, whether, as they had already made clear, the patient was irremediably lost. He demanded a definite answer. Appealed to in this way, the doctors in turn gave the same diagnosis: the patient was doomed and the end would come in the very near future, within two months at most.

" 'There isn't the slightest chance of a cure?' insisted the Baron.

"As I listened to him express himself in this way, I thought for a moment he was going to side with me. The doctors confirmed that in the light of science and all their previous experience, the Baroness could not recover. The oldest physician voiced some qualifications, admitting in vague terms that in the past one had seen some very rare cases of erroneous diagnoses and that one could always hope for the possibility of an exceptional case. It was clear he was speaking like this to spare the Baron's sensibility.

" 'For my part,' he concluded firmly, 'I should consider a cure or even a passing improvement a miracle.'

"The other two having at last concurred with this opinion, the Baron continued:

" 'I thank you, gentlemen. I accept your verdict with sorrow but with resignation. It means that I must become inured to this cruel loss within two months, save for a miraculous intervention I still hope for. Because never— never—' he continued, raising his voice, 'never will I consent to grant the prayer of my wife, whose mind is unhinged by such unendurable suffering. A life is sacred and under no circumstances should be cut short by a human hand under the pretext of pity. Gentlemen physicians, let that be understood.'

" 'A life is sacred,' protested the three doctors in chorus. 'You don't need to remind us, Monsieur le Baron, for it is the first article of our code. We would never agree to cut short that existence, even though the suffering of the patient were a hundred times more acute; even though you, Monsieur le Baron, added your entreaty to hers. Our duty is to protract the pangs of death as long as possible by every means at the disposal of science. We have sworn this oath in the past, and we repeat it.'

" 'I believe you and I thank you,' said the châtelain gravely.

"He invited the old servant to express her feelings too, and she declared with fire that she would rather cut off her arm than cut off or allow anyone to cut off a second of her mistress's life. The Baron concluded, addressing himself to me:

" 'This meeting you asked for has been, then, useless, and it will serve no purpose to prolong it.'

"The doctors left, casting a suspicious look in my direction. And, after having renewed their prescriptions, they gave instructions that no one ever leave within the patient's reach the capsules which were administered to her one by one at long intervals without bringing the faintest relief. It was an unnecessary precaution: the Baron kept the container of capsules under lock and key in his own room.

"After they had gone, the Baron watched me for a long time without a word. Then he broke his silence to request with severity that I stop my visits. I bowed to his will and left the château. There the unhappy woman continued to suffer, yet the serenity of the atmosphere was not disturbed by it, or the joyous twittering of the birds troubled by the frantic signs of her silent fingers.' "

"Old Man," I said, "you did well to warn me your story wasn't exactly cheerful. It has depressed me deeply. The evocation of this moribund creature unable to express her pain except by spasmodic gestures seems cruel. I can only hope for a quick end to her silent agony."

"I am terribly sorry to disappoint you, but this agony was protracted. As a matter of fact, it turned out that the Baroness was still living at the end of the two months set by the doctors—always in the same state, always a prey to racking pain and demanding with more and more frenzied agitation of her hands the deliverance they refused her. I had ceased my visits, as the Baron had requested, but from time to time I had news of the château and its occupants from the interpreter, with whom I was on familiar terms. He enjoyed the Baron's confidence and continued to converse with his wife, if such a means of communication, in which the litanies are endlessly repeated, can be called conversing.

"So I learned that since the time fixed by the professional men had expired several weeks ago, the Baron had decided to appeal to another doctor, a stranger from a neighboring kingdom, whose reputation, great in his own country, was beginning to extend to all Southeast Asia in the wake of almost miraculous cures he was said to have worked. This man not only practiced modern medicine, but also made use of the methods traditional science readily taxes with charlatanry—methods, however, that sometimes produce results where conventional ones have failed. This was just what happened in the Baroness's case."

"Do you mean she was cured? That there was at least an improvement in her condition? That he succeeded in easing her pain?"

"Not altogether, Monsieur. The patient's suffering remained unabated, but one should consider that he brought about a certain betterment of her condition, for after a first session, on the basis of acupuncture, mesmeric passes and incantations, the patient recovered the use of speech."

"Completely?"

"Only intermittently, at certain moments. During one

whole period she went through alternating states of speech and speechlessness. This was what the Baron himself confirmed when, to my great surprise, he came to see me a fortnight after one such period. After his explanation he sank into a morose silence.

" 'What does she say when her tongue is loosened?' I asked.

" 'The same thing as before, in a different language. She moans, she cries, she screams that she is in pain.'

" 'Perhaps this is an encouraging sign,' I said. 'A first step toward recovery.'

" 'Perhaps.'

"Once more he was absorbed in silence. I found his manner odd. I had to wrest his words from him one at a time.

" 'Don't you wish to come to see her?' he asked at last, timidly, as if he were requesting a favor.

" 'You forbade me to.'

" 'I've come to apologize,' he said hastily. 'Your words shocked me. To shorten the life of a beloved seemed and still seems to me an odious act. But I've thought a great deal since then, and I've understood you offered this opinion only because you were moved by excessive charity. If you don't bear me a grudge for my attitude, I beg you earnestly to resume your visits.'

"I promised him to return to the château the very next day. He seemed relieved.

" 'Possibly your presence will do her good, more especially as you'll be able to speak to her without having recourse to the interpreter. She can hear, too. And then,' he added in a tone that betrayed deep distress, 'for me as well, you'll be a source of invaluable comfort. I need it.'

" 'You do seem deeply concerned,' I remarked. 'I pity you with all my heart and I'll make every effort to lighten your burden.'

"And it was true, Monsieur. This man who had always shown admirable equanimity seemed nervous, in poor health, and every now and then his look expressed an anguish that stirred compassion. He almost wept when, with heartfelt thanks, he took leave of me.

" 'You'll see for yourself,' he murmured as he went away. 'I shan't say more to you, but I assure you the house is not very gay.'

"I was pondering his last words the next day as I approached the château and couldn't fend off an irrational fear. Nevertheless, when I reached there, the atmosphere did not seem changed in any way. I knocked at the door softly, careful not to disturb the silence that still prevailed. It was a wise precaution. The servant came to let me in and immediately put a finger to her lips, enjoining me to speak quietly.

" 'She has been silent for a quarter of an hour,' she whispered.

"I observed that she had the same tormented look that I had seen the day before on her master's face.

" 'We are having a little respite,' she continued, 'but it can't last. You'll find Monsieur le Baron at the far end of the garden.'

" 'Mayn't I see her first?'

" 'If you wish. But for the love of heaven, don't show yourself! Don't disturb her. She could immediately fall back into a crisis.'

"Through the door that was barely ajar I saw the patient in the semi-obscurity of a bedroom the windows of which were hermetically sealed. Her position was familiar to me. Stretched out on her bed, her face ravaged, her fingers were feverishly moving in silence as before. I withdrew without making a noise.

" 'She doesn't speak any more?'

" 'Only in crises. More and more frequent, alas!' "

"In *crises,* Old Man?" I interrupted.

"It was the second time she'd used the term, which surprised me too, but I was soon to understand its terrible significance.

"I went into the garden and the servant carefully closed the door behind me. I found the châtelain at the bottom of the garden, in the most remote part of the grounds, behind a quite dense thicket. He was seated in a rustic armchair reading a book. Three or four other volumes were stacked at his feet. He seemed calmer than the day before and smiled faintly when he caught sight of me.

" 'Here is where I have to take refuge when she is in crisis,' he said, using the same word as the servant. 'The library, alas, has become unlivable as well as have the other rooms of the château. Fortunately, her cries don't reach this far and so I've been able to make a haven during the day. But I spend ghastly nights.'

" 'Listening to her?'

" 'Hearing her. When you have had the experience, you'll understand just how painful my situation is. Sometimes my old servant has to come and join me here.'

"Once more he thanked me effusively for being kind

enough to resume my visits and again excused himself insistently for having requested me in the past to interrupt them, giving me the reason I had long since guessed.

" 'After the opinion you had voiced on the fitness of a merciful gesture, I might have supposed that you would possibly have taken the initiative without my consent. I repent of that. I was certainly mistaken. You are incapable of such an act, aren't you?'

" 'Incapable,' I confirmed, not flinching at his look, which had taken on a peculiar intensity.

" 'That is just what I thought.'

"Monsieur, it was only a fleeting impression, but it seemed to me for one brief moment that my reply annoyed him.

"During this conversation he had abandoned his book and we were walking the full length of the garden. He was making an effort to appear sprightly and pretended to be interested in the flowers and birds, but I noticed that his feverishness came back every time we drew near the castle again, that at the same time he was straining his ears to catch the slightest sound that might come from there.

"At one moment, as if justifying his uneasiness, a sharp wail, muffled a little by the walls but perfectly audible, disturbed the quiet of the garden. The Baron jumped, and a terrified light flickered in the pupil of the eye.

" 'I had indeed spoken to you of this. I felt it could not last long. But there it is, starting up again. The crises are more and more frequent.'

"The lugubrious plaint was unceasing, broken by cries and indistinct words resembling entreaties mingled with insults. I must confess, Monsieur, that this awful concert made an excruciating impression on me too."

"Excruciating, Old Man?"

"I don't believe I've ever experienced a sensation so painful. The atmosphere of the château suddenly seemed funereal. The birds circling round us took flight at the first noise to perch in the depths of the garden behind the thicket, where I had found the Baron. He now went in the same direction.

" 'I beg of you, go see her,' he flung at me as he fled. 'Perhaps you'll be able to make her listen to reason. I am not going with you. I have to endure that during all hours of the night. Inside the house it's unbearable.'

"He was right, Monsieur. Inside the house these lamentations were absolutely intolerable."

"Intolerable, really?"

"Unendurable for one's nerves, and I had to summon all my courage to push open the door behind which the woman was now pouring forth her sufferings in an abominable witches' Sabbath. What shall I tell you of this conversation, Monsieur? The placating words I tried to pronounce were soon stifled by a flood of moans, plaints, howls, supplications. After some vain attempts to make myself heard, I had to give up. I went back to the garden and in my turn headed straight toward the protective screen of the grove of trees.

"A little before reaching there, I came upon the old servant, who had dropped on a bench, head in hands.

" 'Did you hear it?' she cried out to me between sobs. 'It is hell.'

"I lingered a few moments to console the poor woman

—to little avail. Then I rejoined the Baron behind the thicket in the haven where, to my great relief, the moaning could no longer be heard. The Baron seemed to have calmed down. He had taken a crust of bread out of his pocket and was throwing crumbs to the birds clustering around him.

" 'Well?' he asked, raising his head.

"I told him my intervention was anything but successful.

" 'That doesn't surprise me. I suppose she repeated the same prayer to you.'

" 'I can still hear her,' I said, shuddering. 'I beseech you, put an end to my suffering, an end to my suffering . . .'

" 'Yes,' said the Baron, his face darkening. *'An end to my suffering.* And I'm forced to endure that funereal litany sometimes all night long. Her voice penetrates the walls of her bedroom and mine. And you don't know the half of it. The foreign doctor, who comes back from time to time, has given me to understand she may permanently recover the use of speech. I don't know whether my health will stand it. . . . And what did you answer?' he added, looking at me strangely.

" 'Impossible to get in a word. Besides, there was nothing to say, was there?' I replied, looking him straight in the eye.

" 'Nothing. You are right,' he declared after a slight hesitation.

"We chatted for a moment, then I took leave of him, after having promised to return the next day.

" 'I thank you,' he said gravely. 'Your presence does me good.' "

"I think the Baron greatly needed solace," I remarked, to urge my storyteller to go on, since he was prolonging one of his pauses.

"He did, Monsieur, and more and more as the situation within the château grew worse. The foreign physician had judged correctly: The Baroness fully recovered the power of speech; in other words, she was in a permanent state of crisis, as those nearest her said. On every one of my visits I was obliged to spend a few minutes in her presence, trying vainly to make myself understood. It was a session that was extremely disagreeable but a duty I could not shirk. The proof being confirmed each time that my presence was of no help to her, I hurried to join the Baron at the far end of the garden, where he now took refuge all day and sometimes a part of the night. He had removed several shelves of his library and sheltered his books in the shed where the garden tools were kept. He always welcomed me with deep satisfaction.

"There I often found the three physicians, whose presence near him was as useful as mine, for his robust constitution was beginning to show signs of stress from the trials imposed upon him. These professional men also spent some painful and useless moments beside the dying woman, moved as I was by a sense of duty. Finally they, too, sought refuge at the bottom of the garden behind the screening thicket. There we could chat calmly for hours at a time, forbidding ourselves to speak of the patient, touching on a wide variety of subjects, trying to change the squire's ideas and, ourselves attempting to forget the atrocious witches' Sabbath of wailing still ringing in our ears.

"One day, however, after I had had to endure the sight of a specially repugnant crisis, I could stand it no longer. I risked putting the question plainly to the poor man— the question we had all been thinking of for some time: namely, whether he was still of the same opinion about the prayer his wife now made day and night. This time he did not seem offended and reflected a long time before replying.

" 'And you?' he asked finally.

" 'More than ever,' I answered. 'I've been thinking just today that it is reprehensible to let this agony be prolonged. I accepted your scruples three months ago, but now circumstances are no longer the same.'

" 'It's true,' he repeated in a subdued voice with great earnestness, 'the circumstances are no longer the same.'

" 'It is undeniable: the circumstances are no longer the same,' cried the three doctors in chorus after having favored me with an approving glance.

"The Baron remained silent for a long while; then he addressed himself to the men of the medical art in a tone of marked gravity:

" 'I must repeat to you the question I asked you three months ago on the course of my wife's malady. Do you still think it is incurable and is bound to have a fatal outcome within a more or less brief period?'

" 'More than ever are we of that opinion,' replied the three doctors in unison.

" 'That there isn't the slightest possibility of recovery?'

" 'Not the shadow of a possibility.'

"I noticed the haste with which they replied, whereas three months earlier they had taken time to reflect. I observed as well that the oldest had refrained from making the faintest allusion to the eventuality of a miracle. The Baron continued:

" 'You had, nonetheless, set a limit of two months, and my wife is still living.'

" 'If one can call that living!' the doctors again exclaimed together.

"They went on, affirming they could have made an error about the length of time, but that there was no mistaking the gravity of the illness. For this they gave excellent reasons, which I've forgotten. The sickness, in their eyes, had already gone into the delirium that precedes death; the patient's extreme agitation was the clearest of symptoms. The mind was already in the beyond. The body would inevitably follow, even if it were granted a new reprieve.

" 'However,' objected the Baron feebly, 'the foreign doctor did obtain one result; it is undeniable: she does speak.'

"They easily demonstrated that the methods of a healer —they pronounced the word with great scorn—might show a certain efficacy when the case concerned nerve action, as did the mutism, but that such methods couldn't have any influence on the root of the disease.

" 'Perfect,' concluded the Baron. 'I have confidence in you and I believe you. Well, gentlemen . . .' "

Then I interrupted my teller of tales, protesting vehemently:

"Old Man, I no longer recognize you. This evening you've put on big wooden shoes—I could hear you coming a long way off. The dire conclusion of your story was transparent at every word. I knew beforehand what the Baron was going to say."

"I believe you knew nothing of the sort, Monsieur," he said harshly. "Be patient until you have heard the discourse he launched into with the doctors and me, in a tone that allowed of no discussion.

" 'Well, gentlemen, you must understand that my opinion, at least, has not changed, despite these new circumstances. I will never consent to shorten the life of a being who is dear to me, and I do not authorize anyone to assume such a responsibility.'

"We lowered our heads. The old servant, who had come to take refuge a moment at the far end of the garden, as she did from time to time, and who had heard our conversation, started in distress and opened her mouth to protest. The Baron bade her be silent with an imperious gesture. And then, his composure recovered, he dismissed us, thanking us once more for our pains before again taking up the pruning of shrubbery he had interrupted on our arrival."

"Old Man, Old Man," I implored, "again you begin to play with me like a cat with a mouse. I am disconcerted, but on reflection I forgive you. Human nature isn't as black as your recital had let me imagine. *Mea culpa.* If the

Baron's torment was as you've described it, one can only bow before such a courageous resolution."

"That was my feeling, Monsieur, and also that of the doctors. Although we were now all four unanimous in wishing that an end be made to the dying woman's torment, we couldn't help but admire the firmness of spirit of her husband, for whom we felt profound compassion.

"I pitied him to such a degree that I felt an immense relief when, a few days after that conversation, I learned of the decease of the Baroness."

"You behold me relieved too," I said with a sigh. "The martyrdom of that poor woman lasted all too long for my taste. I assume that the decease was natural, after the husband's categorical declaration."

"In the town nothing was thought more natural, given the patient's state of health. Besides, the three doctors were there to attest that death had come the way they had been predicting for a long time, and they did not deny themselves this vindication, I assure you. They signed all the necessary certificates. As for me, still mindful of the words pronounced by the Baron, I couldn't permit myself to ascribe any other cause to the death than disease. So I sided at first entirely with public opinion."

"Entirely, at first? Does it mean that later on you changed your mind?"

"I had to, Monsieur. Sometime after the funeral service, which was performed before a numerous company come to express their sympathy to the Baron, I received word from him, asking me to stop by to see him. He had, he asserted, a serious revelation to make to me.

"I didn't fail to respond to his invitation, quite intrigued by the tone of his letter. I found the château once more filled with the serenity of bygone days. The birds had again taken possession of the whole garden, and the wide-open windows of the château let in the bright sunlight of spring. The Baron received me at the threshold and asked me to enter his library, where all his books had been replaced on their shelves. He had resumed his habits of former days as well as his peaceful air.

" 'I've been anxious to see you in order to set my conscience free,' he said after the usual exchange of courtesies. 'You shall be the only one to know the truth about the decease of my unhappy wife, but more than anyone else, you are capable of understanding me and, I hope, of absolving me.'

" 'Am I to assume . . . ?'

"Slowly he nodded his head.

" 'I am the one,' he said. 'All at once it occurred to me that I couldn't do otherwise. And then, one evening, I simply left the vial of capsules within arm's reach. For the first time in a long while she smiled and I felt a great contentment. Her moaning died away in the night.'

"I remained for some time at a loss. Then I assured him that I understood his gesture perfectly, that, as he knew, in his place I would have done it long before, that I didn't even see a reason for pardon, and that if there existed a God capable of judging the feelings that move us, He would be the first to give him absolution.

" 'This is what I believe,' he said, 'but I like to hear it confirmed by a man of religion, even though he profess Doubt.'

"I couldn't, however, keep from showing some surprise

115

at the fact that he had so suddenly gone back on his fierce determination to let nature take its course.

" 'A new fact arose,' he said after some hesitation. 'From you, I don't need to hide anything.'

" 'A worsening of her illness?'

" 'Not that. But the foreign physician came back. He hadn't shared the opinion of the other three.'

" 'He had foreseen a possible cure?'

" 'Oh, without committing himself,' protested the Baron quickly. 'He didn't formulate a diagnosis, far from it. He held out only an extremely vague possibility.'

"He stopped abruptly and I had the impression he was biting his tongue, as if he regretted the words he had just spoken.

" 'What I retained from the doctor's statements was that my wife might linger a long while—a very long while, years perhaps, with her unbearable suffering. That is what decided me.'

" 'I understand all the better,' I said after a silence.

"And then, having reflected again, I once more gave him a sort of absolution, since he seemed to wish it. He expressed his gratification at my having thus eased his conscience.

" 'I don't need to recommend discretion to you,' he said again. 'You are the only one to know the truth. Even my old servant has suspected nothing. I put the vial in its hiding place at dawn.'

"Soon I left him. It was the servant who accompanied me to the wrought-iron gate of the château. As I've told you, she was a faithful servant, whose devotion to her master and mistress had never been found wanting. I

116

offered her my condolences, as to a member of the family, and we exchanged some commonplaces.

" 'A great misfortune,' I said to her, 'but, for her, a deliverance.'

" 'A deliverance, most certainly, and, too, for M. le Baron. One might say that the sudden end has been a benediction from heaven for him. He had already endured a long Calvary, but he couldn't have withstood the hell this devil of a sorcerer had got into his head to inflict on him—supposedly to comfort the wife.'

"I was on the point of leaving her. Taken aback, I changed my mind in order to ask her for details.

" 'Had the foreign doctor, then, prescribed a new treatment?'

" 'Didn't M. le Baron tell you about it? After his last visit, this devil decreed the patient needed fresh air. According to him, it was of vital importance. He demanded that the windows of her bedroom be kept wide open all the time, night and day.'

" 'The windows that open on the garden?' I asked.

" 'Exactly. M. le Baron consented and stood it for a whole day. The poor man wandered like a soul in torment through this garden, which was now pierced with howls and maledictions. His last refuge had been denied him. If she hadn't died in the night, I believe he would have gone mad.'

"There you have my story, Monsieur. And I think the old servant was right: he would have gone insane. He suffered too much. Don't you think so?"

"Very likely, Old Man," I admitted, nodding my head. "Endurance of pain has its limits."

# Compassion
## Service

# 1

W<small>OULD IT PLEASE YOU</small>, Monsieur, to listen to the story of an adventure I have kept intact in my memory? Perhaps it will disappoint you, since it doesn't present any of those highly spiced touches in which you seem to take such keen pleasure, yet I like to tell it, for it concerns me quite intimately."

I had hunted for my centenarian in all the spots where I thought there was a chance of running across him, even in the dens he sometimes frequents, on a night that was again one of anguished sterility for me, coming at the end of an interminable series of similar nights feverishly devoted to the search for an interesting subject. My pursuit of the storyteller proving fruitless, I walked the streets at random, musing bitterly that literary critics ought to erect statues of solid gold to us, the tellers of tales, the novelists, who month after month kindly deliver to them priceless treasures on which they can comment.

Luck guided my steps toward the café where I habitually inveigled him into reeling off his memories after I had bought him a drink. There he was, seated on the shabby plush, at the very same table at which we had already spent some nights tête-à-tête, as though a premonition had warned him I had a pressing need of his services. A glance at my drawn face undoubtedly confirmed for him that such was the case and he proffered those services even before I had opened my mouth to greet him. I sat down without taking time to remove my coat, and I, too, scorned the usual polite formalities.

"I beg of you, I beseech you, Old Man, tell me the story. You're too modest; I'm sure any adventure that involves you so intimately can't be pointless."

He received this homage with a nod of approval and began:

"Monsieur, not only does this story concern me, not only am I the modest hero, but it also marks the turning point in my life that led me to renounce the world and its vanities. For me it was an intermediary step before entering upon the religious life."

"The religion of Doubt," I remarked.

"Yes, Monsieur, the religion of Doubt, sad, colorless for pagans, radiant for the initiated.

"The adventure begins in a somber period of my life. I was a lawyer, as you know, a lawyer without cases, and the profession no longer interested me; every day it became a bit more repugnant. I was poor; I earned barely enough to live on, and I suffered from this foolishly, not yet having acquired the philosophy that permits one to be contemptuous of material goods. Besides, I had had several sentimental disappointments, one after another, that had strongly affected me for the same silly reason, so that I walked and walked, day and night, a frustrated soul with the depressing consciousness of being a failure."

"Your disposition seems to me to have undergone a happy change, Old Man."

"True, Monsieur. But at that period I was so melancholy that every night I contemplated putting an end to such an aimless existence."

"Infamous rogue!" I muttered under my breath. "There you are, about to take one of those crooked paths on which you revel. Why must I listen to these unhealthy stories, all turning upon the idea of destruction?"

He must have read a certain distaste in my expression, for he added:

"Monsieur, if it would reassure you, I might reveal to you at the outset that my adventure, though beginning on this gloomy note, ends otherwise."

"You've set my mind at ease, Old Man."

"I congratulate myself, too, for having escaped those morbid temptations and for being here this evening, very much alive and thankful for this grace in spite of being a hundred years old. This I owe to a fortuitous circumstance that caused me to recover spiritual peace and, principally, to a man whose memory I shall never revere enough. Well then, if you'll permit me, I'll go on with my narrative.

123

"I envisaged putting an end to my days and was carefully examining—my mind was methodical, even though troubled—different modes of suicide, without ever settling on any one of them, when, quite by chance, while I was distractedly scanning the town gazette, my attention was arrested by a headline in boldface: COMPASSION SERVICE, followed by a telephone number. I read the notice. The journalist praised the merits of an association of voluntary benefactors ready, day and night, to receive the calls of persons in despair, to console them by the power of the word and help them recover their zest for life.

"This notice seemed to me a sign of fate and I decided to try the venture. That very evening I called the number indicated. I must admit to you that I did it with a certain hesitancy and that I didn't put any great faith in this service, which I had already heard of elsewhere. In my case, it seemed to me, every word of consolation would be empty. Sin of pride.

"I was mistaken, Monsieur, as you'll see. The voice of a woman, evidently a switchboard operator, answered me. She didn't ask me a single question and simply requested me to be patient for a few moments. The wait wasn't long, heaven be praised, for, doubt coming over me again, I hesitated over hanging up or not. I was about to do so when I heard another voice, a man's.

" 'Speaking, Compassion Service. What can I do for you?'

"I waited a moment without replying, but it wasn't anguish that made me mute. Quite the contrary. Strangely enough, the mere sound of the voice brought me hope. It was a calm voice, rather soft, yet with a hint of authority. As I listened, a word instinctively came to my mind to describe it: serenity.

" 'There's no need to be afraid to speak,' the voice went on as my silence continued. 'I'm here to listen to you and to help you, if I can.'

" 'I am alone, forsaken, disgusted with life,' I finally murmured. 'In the palm of my hand I hold an ampule containing a fatal poison I intend to swallow.' "

"Was it true?" I interrupted, eyeing him suspiciously.

"No, Monsieur, it wasn't. There was nothing at all in the palm of my hand. I've told you I hadn't yet chosen my mode of suicide."

"The eternal actor," I murmured softly. "I'd have bet on that."

"It was what, in the realm of Shandong, we call a lie of politeness."

"Of politeness?"

"It would have been highly inappropriate to let him think I had disturbed him for a triviality. Actually, I wasn't paying much attention to the sense of my words. What I wished was to hear him speak, to hear the sound of that voice so marked by a serenity nothing seemed able to shake. Thus I fell silent again, my breathing audible."

"Still pretending to gasp for breath the better to impress him," I murmured charitably to myself.

"I wasn't disappointed. The voice resumed:

" 'One is never so alone as one thinks. Open your eyes. Look around you. To do so attentively is often to find a friendly presence.'

"That's all I remember of a rather long speech the man

made. I wasn't paying any more attention to the sense of his words than to my own. The quality of his voice was enough to soothe me. He concluded by making me promise at least to put off my plan of suicide, which I did, and to call him the next day at the same hour, or even earlier if I wished. If he was not there or was busy, someone would answer without fail. Compassion Service was at the disposition of the unhappy round the clock. I told him I preferred to continue with him, which seemed to bring him keen satisfaction. Then I made bold to ask him his name. He laughed quietly.

" 'It's not our practice to divulge our real names,' he said. 'Here I'm called M. Vincent. That's the surname my friends and collaborators have chosen for me.'

"You must understand, Monsieur, that by 'M. Vincent' I'm translating as best I can a name hard to pronounce in your language. It's that of a holy man in the realm of Shandong who spent his life in helping the unfortunate."

"I understand," I said. "Continue."

"That was my first contact with this man. Only later was I to understand and appreciate better the immense goodness, the deep knowledge of the human heart, the infinite compassion with which he brooded over the sorrows of his brothers and sisters. I called the Service the following day at the same hour in the hope of finding the same interlocutor again. I wasn't disappointed. The serene voice of M. Vincent answered. He made some remarks similar to those of the day before and we said good-by after I had made him the same promise.

"This performance was repeated for almost a week. Every evening the conversation brought me solace, but a solace so fleeting that it was dissipated at the end of a few hours. After that, I fell back into melancholy until the next evening's conversation, a conversation that for me consisted above all in listening to M. Vincent, my loneliness and moroseness inspiring in me only a few bitter phrases.

"At the end of a week I confessed to him this state of mind, taking care not to annoy him, insisting that it was certainly because of my own unworthiness if the sort of cure he had undertaken couldn't yet be considered successful. He remained silent a long while. I surmised he was thinking things over.

" 'I suggest that we meet,' he said finally. 'In you I have a foreboding of a serious case for which consolation by telephone cannot suffice. It's not usual, but every now and then we pay a visit to one of our clients especially afflicted.' "

"Just a minute, Old Man," I said. "Is 'client' exactly the term he used?"

"That and no other, Monsieur. I answered that I'd be delighted by such a meeting, which would unquestionably be very profitable."

" 'Better still,' he resumed after having again thought it over, 'why don't you come here to pay us a visit? You've led me to understand that your work leaves you quite a lot of leisure and, in spite of your temporary depression, I feel you might be interested in our modest establishment.'

"I accepted this invitation eagerly. For some days, in fact, I had been torn by curiosity to know the place from which this voice emanated.

" 'I'm here every day,' continued M. Vincent, 'in the

afternoon and a great part of the evening. But sometimes I come to take my turn in the mornings, though calls are infrequent. So come tomorrow morning; we'll be able to chat quietly without being disturbed.'

"As I learned later, that was one of his characteristics. While his other colleagues of the Service took turns listening, M. Vincent was, in a way, a permanent member, devoting to it the greatest part of his time.

"The next day, then, at the appointed hour, with my heart pounding a little, I rang the bell at the door of Compassion Service, the premises of which were an apartment in a faded mansion. M. Vincent himself opened the door.

" 'I was expecting you,' he said simply. 'Welcome.'

"He was a man in his sixties, of average height, a little portly, with a certain unctuousness in his manner that at first glance might have made one take him for an ecclesiastic. His ruddy complexion, his quick eye, his smile, suggested a person on whom adversity could have little hold.

"Our conversation bore out my impression that he always took an optimistic view of life. He didn't talk about my troubles. For my part, I felt no need to bare them. After an exchange of polite commonplaces, he said:

" 'Do you wish to see our little establishment? It is still quite modest, but we plan to enlarge it. Such as it is, it already affords us much satisfaction.'

"In making this proposal, he had the happy look of a property owner doing the honors of a private domain of which he is proud. I was thrilled, as if on the threshold of a temple hallowed in mystery. However, there was nothing forbidding in the premises through which he took me.

" 'Compassion Service occupies five offices,' he said, pointing them out to me, 'plus a little recess for our switchboard operator. She doesn't come mornings and the line is plugged in for whoever is on duty. I myself take turns very often, as I've indicated to you. The room you see there is my office. I like it. I profit by the quiet of the morning to make notes or do my correspondence. You can see that it's neat and quite comfortable. These two qualities are indispensable to us. We must have order because from time to time we must treat and pursue a great number of serious matters, some quite complicated. And we must have comfort because, spending a large part of the day, sometimes even of the night, here, we would find the hours—I, especially—rather irksome if we were not properly set up.'

"In fact, Monsieur, I found the appointments not only comfortable, but stylish. I remarked on this to him and he was appreciative. Every detail of the furniture seemed to have been studied for the delight of the eye as well as for its utility. The office was in a period favored at the time of our ancient sovereign, different from your Louis Quinze, but just as elegant. The easy chairs were similar in style, but more comfortable, deeper and with plump cushions that invited one to sit down and relax.

" 'I was the one who had the furniture changed,' declared my host, gratified by my evident admiration. 'In the past the office had horrible tables of white wood barely acceptable for a kitchen; and hard chairs that caused un-bearable stiffness after we had listened a long time.'

" 'I should never have imagined,' I said, 'that the offices of Compassion Service would be so pleasant.' "

"Is 'pleasant,' Old Man, really the term the sight of these premises inspired in you?"

"And which M. Vincent himself used along with others equally apt: order, comfort, intimacy, harmony—that is what was suggested by the sight of what he called 'our modest establishment.'

" 'My young friend,' M. Vincent replied to my rather naïve remark with a condescending smile, 'to withstand all the sadnesses and horrors we hear about in this place, a pleasant atmosphere is indispensable, and we all strive to create it. You would be wrong to confuse us with austere benefactors. Nor are we ever bored, I assure you, neither I nor any of my collaborators, and when we have any leisure we aren't above amusing ourselves with in-nocuous games.'

"He opened a wall cupboard and showed me a number of games arranged on shelves: cards, chess, checkers—games in which simple minds can take pleasure.

" 'Thus the time passes more quickly, even when the calls are infrequent,' he explained. 'This happens when the kingdom goes through a period of calm and prosperity that is reflected in every individual. And then each of us indulges in his favorite diversion. For my part, I very much enjoy chess. Some of my collaborators prefer bridge, and I sometimes join them when they need a fourth. In that case, it is the dummy who is on service to answer a possible call, unless one of us is personally required, which necessitates our interrupting the game. If you think these soothing distractions could in no case be harmful to the exercise of our ministry, you are correct.'

"After showing me the inside of another cupboard, containing tea and a tea service, he insisted:

" 'These moments of relaxation are necessary. How could we console desperate persons if we ourselves were dispirited? The humor, the *joie de vivre* we try to arouse in others, we must first experience ourselves to the very depths of our souls.' "

"Words of a sage, Old Man. This M. Vincent seems to me to have been a discerning philosopher."

"A remarkable man from every point of view, Monsieur. When I came to know him better, I understood why his colleagues of Compassion Service recognized him as their chief. He denied that he was, always calling them his collaborators. He was goodness itself and, in addition to this, charity and wisdom. No one in the bosom of this team possessed more than he the art of concerning himself with the woes of others."

"Truly concerning himself?" I interrupted.

"At times even becoming impassioned. I've seen instances of this.

"We continued the visit. The five offices were all furnished in the same way, with a few variations that, as M. Vincent called to my attention, reflected the personality of the occupant. A thick carpet deadened the noise of our steps. The rather narrow windows, framed with hangings in warm colors, let only a little daylight filter through. He seized this pretext to switch on the electricity and invited me to observe the soft light thrown

by the lamps placed on each table in the room, a light
diffused by a large shade that didn't tire the eyes."

"A haven of repose," I commented.

"That was somewhat the impression I had as my host
pointed out the large cabinets covering an entire parti-
tion of the office. I admired the rustic style, which didn't
clash with the rest of the furniture. He laughed softly and
rubbed his hands together with a look of satisfaction.

" 'Nobody would suspect that these teak panels conceal our precious records,' he said. 'The camouflage was
cleverly carried out by a cabinetmaker, one of our clients
whose taste for life and for his craft I had succeeded in
restoring. The old filing cabinets were an eyesore. If you
look carefully, you'll see they are still there, but one
doesn't notice them.'

"He pushed back the folding doors of one cabinet and
revealed a metal file, one drawer on top of another, such
as one sees in business offices. He pulled out one of the
drawers and showed me scores of tightly packed index
cards.

" 'More than any other, an organization like ours,' he
explained, 'needs systematic record-keeping. We make it
a special point to keep complete up-to-date statistics based
on the thousands of calls we receive each month. And so
I have only to glance at this index to know that, on the
average, out of a hundred calls there are—just read for
yourself, my young friend.'

"I read: fifty marital dramas, thirty cases of loneliness,
ten sexual problems, ten of alcoholism.

" 'These documents are extremely valuable to us,' he

concluded. 'You may examine some of them if you are interested.'

"I looked over various statistical tables. From these I learned that women's calls were far more frequent than those of men—in some years as many as eight women to two men. I saw that those over sixty represented barely one percent as opposed to thirty percent for those under twenty-five. I learned that love tragedies were more frequent among homosexuals, according to a percentage that I apologize for having forgotten today. And so, Monsieur, in a matter of minutes, I became familiar with a field that until that time had been completely foreign to me."

"Which seems to have brought you an intense intellectual satisfaction?"

"At the same time my curiosity was so whetted that I felt a great desire to learn more.

" 'As you can realize,' resumed M. Vincent, closing the file cabinet, 'I am far from being an enemy of progress. Believe me, I appreciate everything modern techniques can bring us in the way of convenience, eliminating loss of time, petty cares, and needless fatigue. You haven't yet seen the ingenuity of our telephonic combined sets. We're rather proud of them. Of course, it's no work of genius. A simple little gadget, as they say in the West, but it's extremely practical.'

"The gadget, Monsieur, was a curved arm of metal fastened to the telephone itself that one could cradle between the neck and the shoulder, thus freeing both hands to take notes and occasionally leaf through the pages of a memorandum while listening. It's in use, I believe, in many offices.

" 'We aren't the ones who invented it,' admitted M. Vincent. 'We have simply perfected it, after having studied different curvatures and covered the metal arm with velvet. If I may say so without bragging, I myself worked a long time before discovering the profile giving the greatest ease, and I had one made—this one—for my own use, according to measure, since my neck is a little thick and the current model didn't entirely suit me. Look, my friend, here is the listening position.'

"His eyes shone with a peculiar brilliance as he lolled back in the armchair, after having settled the instrument, which, as he pointed out to me, fitted the hollow between his neck and shoulder perfectly. Then he stretched out his arms along the arms of the chair and appeared to me the picture of beatitude.

" 'In this way, even after a long time I don't experience any bodily fatigue, which an uncomfortable position causes and which slows the quickness of thought. So I've been able to stay on the phone two hours at a time, listening to the plaints of a young girl who swore to me she had a razor blade in her hand and had decided to cut her veins because of an unhappy love affair. Exactly two hours, my young friend,' he insisted vehemently, 'and, would you believe it, at the end of this trial, I didn't suffer the slightest cramp or the least stiffness.' "

The Old Man paused briefly. I opened my mouth to speak, but he didn't give me time enough and went on:

"M. Vincent replaced the instrument carefully, got up,

and continued to do the honors of the establishment with the utmost courtesy.

" 'Now you have a clearer idea of our service,' he said finally, 'but in the morning you can't appreciate what it's really like. The atmosphere of work is missing; the life is not there. You must catch sight of us, of me and my colleagues, at the peak of activity, that is, in the evening, in order to breathe the real atmosphere.'

" 'I would love that,' I confessed.

"It was true, Monsieur. My curiosity was only partly satisfied. It was a little as if I had gone to a theater on a day when there was no performance.

" 'But is that possible?' I asked.

" 'We aren't in the habit of receiving guests when we are busy, but you are exceptionally understanding. I'll speak to my colleagues about it and I am sure they'll have no objection. So telephone me tomorrow and we'll make an appointment.'

"On that note, Monsieur, I took leave of him and left the place with an odd feeling of nostalgia. It seemed to me that depression was about to descend upon me the minute I set foot outside."

I profited from a silence on the part of my nocturnal storyteller to ask the question I had had in mind a moment ago:

"Old Man, I've fully appreciated the vivid description you've given me of this Service and its principal moving spirit. I have especially admired the patience and serenity of M. Vincent, who could remain in his easy chair without budging, his ear glued to the telephone, listening to the lamentations of a young girl on the point of cutting her veins and who, in his own words, felt no stiffness at the end of this trial. And the young girl, Old Man? What happened to her?"

"My word, Monsieur, he forgot to tell me of her fate. His mind was elsewhere. Mine, too, for I didn't think to ask him the question."

## 2

The Old Man was silent, absorbed in one of those meditative pauses he affects. I, too, mused a long while, trying to take in the strange atmosphere of Compassion Service. Then, his silence dragging on, I decided to rouse him.

"I assume you didn't fail to call M. Vincent the next day?"

"That very evening, Monsieur. I couldn't wait. As I had felt, the relief my visit had brought me was quickly dissipated and I had spent a bad afternoon, thoughts of death still revolving in my head.

"I dialed the telephone number, now inscribed on my brain in indelible characters, and asked to speak to M. Vincent immediately. The operator replied that he was on the phone; would I like to speak to another member of the Service? I'd prefer holding the line, even a long while if necessary, which I did. In the prolonged silence I imagined him sunk in his easy chair, listening unwearied to the confidence of a despairing person other than myself, and I was envious. At last I heard a click, then his voice.

" 'I'm sorry about this delay,' he said, 'but you must understand that I must devote myself to all those who are unhappy and that I don't have the right to disappoint them. The person with whom I was just conversing deserved my compassion as much as any other and I hope I've helped him.'

"That man, Monsieur, possessed as much perspicacity as goodness. He had guessed my state of mind. I was ashamed of my egoism and excused myself for my impatience, attributing it to the dreadful melancholy that was undermining me once more.

"He didn't comment, thought for a few seconds, then:

" 'Come at once,' he said, and he added in a low voice, as though to himself: 'Unquestionably it's the best remedy.'

"I quickly hurried toward the building of Compassion Service. With what emotion I remember that evening to this day! M. Vincent himself received me at the threshold.

" 'Delighted to see you again so soon,' he said to me, 'and here, for fear I forget it, take this key to our apartment. It will let you come pay us a visit even when we are all busy, which sometimes happens. In that way you'll feel somewhat at home.'

"I was moved to tears by this mark of confidence. He brushed aside my thanks and once more led me into the interior of the building. Then he introduced me quickly to four of his associates. Two, a man and a woman, were relaxing in front of their offices, the man reading a detective story, the woman knitting.

"  'One can't call it the rush hour this evening,' the woman remarked. 'I haven't had a call yet.'

"We exchanged a few friendly words, and I saw with joy the same expression of serenity that had struck me on M. Vincent's face.

"The other two were in full swing. My host made a sign to me to keep silent and the amenities were confined to a quick wave of the hand. After that they resumed the listening posture of which M. Vincent had given me a glimpse, the body cozily nestled in the depths of the easy chair, the phone cradled between neck and shoulder, the arms stretched out on the chair arms, the muscles relaxed, with an expression of calmness on the face that aroused envy. For a few seconds I remained in contemplation before the last listener. He was keeping a thoughtful silence while nodding his head gently; then, when the very faint buzzing of the receiver stopped, he uttered a few words in a gentle voice. I made out almost the same phrases M. Vincent had addressed to me after my first call: One is never so alone as one thinks. It is enough to know how to look around one.

"  'Come,' whispered my host, 'one mustn't disturb him in the exercise of his duties. Nothing is more annoying. I know this from my own experience.'

"We entered his office. I noticed the heavy curtains carefully drawn, letting no light filter through and no noise penetrate from outside. Instinctively, I walked stealthily—useless precaution, for the floor covering muffled the slightest sound. The lamp of the office spread a carpet of diffused light, inviting meditation and pleasant reverie. The waxed panels of the cabinets evoked the magic of mirrors."

" '*Là tout n'est qu'ordre et beauté, luxe, calme et volupté,*' "* I murmured.

"That was my impression, Monsieur. The room's soft atmosphere seemed marked with a serenity even more enveloping than it had been in the morning.

"However, M. Vincent remained standing and was silently watching me, apparently reflecting.

" 'Don't you wish to try this chair?' he said finally. 'You'll see for yourself how comfortable it is. I detect from your look that you're dying of envy.'

"This diabolical man had again detected a desire I hadn't dared put into words. I didn't have to be urged. I sat down timidly at first, then with growing assurance. I ensconced myself, as I had seen him do. I felt at ease. He approved of my position.

" 'Very good. Pick up the telephone.'

"I took the phone off the hook, placed the receiver against my ear, and realized with a naïve pleasure that the instrument wedged itself between my neck and shoulder. I felt better and better.

" 'It seems to have been made for you,' remarked M. Vincent. 'We have almost the same measurements. With just a tiny alteration it would be perfect. Relax; stretch out your arms. My word, my young friend, one would say you've done this all your life.'

"I was terribly flattered by this compliment. And yet instantaneously a shadow dimmed my contentment.

---

* *"There all is but order and beauty, luxury, calm and pleasure."* —Baudelaire

" 'Alas!' I murmured. 'It's only a game.'

"And I replaced the instrument with a sigh. He stayed there a while, watching me silently.

" 'I must leave for a few minutes,' he said at last. 'An urgent errand in the neighborhood.'

"I got up, greatly disappointed. He made me sit down again with quiet authority.

" 'Wait for me here. We haven't had time to chat. I'll be back in less than ten minutes. If by any chance there's a call in my absence, there's no need to answer. The operator will transfer it to one of my colleagues.'

"With these words he left. I remained alone, huddled in the hollow of the easy chair, in a rather strange state of exaltation. I had an inkling that an event of great importance was about to happen, a trial I feared but at the same time wished for with all my heart.

"This presentiment, Monsieur, wasn't wrong. Minutes after his departure a red signal lighted up in the office and the telephone bell rang. My nerves were so tense that I jumped, though the sound was rather pleasing to the ear. There, too, M. Vincent's aesthetic sense had led him to replace the usual piercing jolt by a melodious purring. I made myself calm down. I listened to the ringing with my whole soul. Its softness seemed an incitement to pluck a sort of forbidden fruit.

"The ring resounded a second, a third time. My muscles had tensed. 'No need to answer,' M. Vincent had said with a careless air; 'the operator will pass on the call to another.' Was that what he had really meant? A kind of smile had been playing about his lips as he had spoken those words. It was certainly not a prohibition. On the contrary, wasn't it an oblique invitation?

"At the fourth ring, Monsieur, I jumped—a naked reflex. I didn't wait for it to end. My hand reached for the phone. I was suddenly panic-stricken for fear the operator would lose patience and switch the call to another office. What a ridiculous feeling! But it had made a shiver go through my body. I had been ashamed of my inertia as though of a guilty cowardice. It seemed to me I was about to defy Providence and miss the opportunity of my life.

"Then I took the receiver off the hook. I stuck it between neck and shoulder, where the listening part fit naturally against my ear. I didn't hear a word—only the sound of labored breathing. The desperate person was there, panting, at the end of the line.

" 'Hooked like a fish on the bait,' I murmured in spite of myself.

"He wasn't about to give up listening if I put him at ease. I myself breathed more freely, lolled back in the depths of the lounge chair, and extended my arms. I cast a furtive look around me. I was quite alone.

" 'Compassion Service speaking,' I said in a voice into which I did my utmost to distill all the serenity with which I began to feel imbued. 'What can I do for you?' "

The Old Man grew silent, doubtless thinking he had reached an essential step in his story. He didn't stop watching me intently, a hint of suspicion in his look, as if to find out whether he had successfully conveyed the kind of enthusiasm he himself seemed to have been experiencing some moments before and that had impelled him to act out the scene, curling up like a cat on the old bench, stretching out his arms on the table with an air of ecstasy. A bit disconcerted by what appeared to me excessive emotion out of proportion to a trivial incident, I remained silent, which could just as well mean a failure to understand as deep thoughtfulness. He resigned himself, a little vexed, to explaining himself more clearly.

"Don't you understand, Monsieur, the importance of this event for me? That was how my cure began. I found peace of mind again. Bless the reflex that impelled me to surmount my fear and pick up the receiver. From that moment on, I never felt alone again. I was incorporated into the family of Compassion Service, in whose bosom I was to spend years of happiness in an ambiance of calm and relaxation so difficult to discover in our days, my heart warmed by the friendship of my colleagues, and my mind constantly kept on the alert by the appeals for help and the confessions of those in despair. You don't believe me?"

"Quite the contrary, Old Man, I readily believe you. I know they must have been years full of enrichment."

"Indeed they were, Monsieur. But I go back to that first evening when, thanks to the fortuitous absence of M. Vincent—at least I still believed it fortuitous—I plunged into the water.

" 'What can I do for you?' I had said. The breathing of the unknown person became even shorter. I seemed to hear at the end of the wire the beating of a heart. And then, finally, his voice—the voice of my first client—and from that instant on he began to speak without stopping, in short, jerky phrases punctuated with sighs. I did not pay close attention to his confession. I retained only a few words and got ready to intervene when he gave me the opportunity. 'When one has to do with a desperate man who is garrulous,' so M. Vincent had taught me in the course of a preceding conversation, 'one must not interrupt him. One must let him speak his speech until he is forced to be silent, having exhausted the list of his woes.'

"That's what happened with my man. After about a quarter of an hour, he ended by saying he was alone, that he had lost his taste for living, and had decided to put an end to his life. Or something like that. It was a classic case that recalled my own, and I didn't have to make any effort to find and pronounce the words of consolation I had already heard: 'One is never so alone as one thinks. Look around you,' et cetera. What joy, Monsieur, after I had spoken in this way for a while, to sense that the unknown man was growing calm. Then he declared in a steadier voice:

" 'It has done me good to talk with you and listen to you. I feel stronger. I promise you to reflect further before carrying out the final act.'

"It was a success. After he had hung up, I remained in the same position for a moment, the instrument still glued to my ear. I was roused from my reverie only by M. Vincent's voice. He had entered noiselessly and heard the end of our conversation.

" 'You've brought it off very well,' he said.

"I thought so myself, but the appreciation of such an expert was infinitely precious to me.

"He added:

" 'I hoped you would take that initiative. It was a sort of test. Now that you have proved yourself, don't you wish to enter our Service?'

"I think you have guessed, Monsieur, it was my dearest wish, an ambition born on my first visit but that I hardly had dared confess to myself. I felt that my salvation lay in this, and I told him so. He agreed.

" 'I am sure, too, that joining our Service will do you enormous good.' "

I couldn't keep from exclaiming and letting my raconteur know of the emotion M. Vincent's offer prompted in me.

"A great benefit for you, Old Man. I believe it without doubt. I understand that you must have experienced an immense relief in discovering beings more hopeless than yourself, but hadn't M. Vincent thought, too, of the help you yourself had the power to give unhappy people? And you, weren't you uneasy about this aspect of the problem?"

"That aspect didn't completely escape us, Monsieur. The proof is that M. Vincent so continued:

" 'I have been judging you from our very first conversation and I believe we have many points in common. I myself, my young friend, like you, was once a person without hope. I must tell you that it is here I've found consolation and have escaped from my frightful loneliness. What is more, as all my colleagues will testify when you know them better, I have been quite successful in the art of comforting the unhappy. There's no reason why you shouldn't achieve the same successes, perhaps some even greater.' "

"Fine, Old Man, I feel relieved of a great burden."

"I protested politely, for form's sake, but I sensed that a calling had been born. And that, Monsieur, is how I entered Compassion Service and came to know spiritual peace.

"I began the exercise of my ministry in the office of M. Vincent, sitting opposite him, while waiting for the room intended for me to be suitably furnished. It was the rule of that institution. Every newcomer first went through a stage of some weeks in company with an elder from whose counsel he could thus profit. I had a telephone of my own and, of course, an easy chair.

"So it was I served my apprenticeship, arduous and exalting at the same time. I familiarized myself with the infinite variety of calls. At times, these appeals presented no particular interest but could be answered routinely. We had only to listen to the litany of small frustrations, momentary despondency, nothing that stirred our pity to the point of making us surpass ourselves. When it was like this, when it sufficed for us to speak some banal words of encouragement to hear our interlocutor overflow with thanks and hang up after the solemn promise not to think any longer of doing something stupid . . ."

"In short, when you didn't have much to sink your teeth into," I interrupted a bit nervously.

". . . the evenings were in danger of becoming monotonous. Certain colleagues, among the youngest in the Service, showed a slight boredom and, between calls, would start a card game. M. Vincent himself never grew tired of listening fervently, even to trifles. He professed that there was always something to glean in the most

145

insignificant cases, and he imbued me with that conception of his ministry, which he would sometimes call an art."

"But I presume M. Vincent himself, like you, like all of you, must have preferred the cases a little out of the ordinary."

"Obviously, Monsieur. And, above all, above everything else, we became attached to persons who, in the jargon of the Service, we called our regular clients, as opposed to fortune's haphazard ones—those whom we could follow and who immediately demanded to speak with Monsieur ——— and not with just an anonymous member of the Service. We all had our surnames."

"Did you become attached to any of these clients?"

"One, Monsieur, and very soon—a woman who undoubtedly deserves special mention. I don't wish to annoy you by giving you a random fact that has no relation to my personal adventure. But in that relationship, let me say that from the moment she insistently asked to speak to me—me and no other—I felt myself finally admitted to a full membership in Compassion Service. There I glided through peaceful days for several years, as I've told you, and even became one of the pillars of the organization. That is my story, Monsieur. I had warned you that it ends in the happiest way in the world."

## 3

My Asian centenarian, my nocturnal muse, with his parchment skin and smooth pate, watched me silently beneath half-closed lids with a ghost of a Mephistophelian smile the significance of which I had known for some time. He pretended to have finished his account, after having treacherously enticed me by a remark made in a slyly casual manner. *She undoubtedly deserves a special mention,* he had said. "Old rogue," I thought. "Once again you're trying to make me beg you." Then, aloud:

"Your marvelous adventure has intrigued me, Old Man, and I would gladly spend hour after hour listening to you, so expert are you in the art of narrative. Didn't you lead me to understand that the regular client you mentioned might be one of those exceptional cases to which the team of Compassion Service attaches so great a price?"

His smile widened.

"Exceptional, no, Monsieur, even commonplace, but curious because of certain fortuitous circumstances."

"Then tell me of these circumstances, Old Man, I beg of you. The night is young and your stories are more interesting than all the spectacles this city offers."

This praise, heightened by a fresh round of drinks, spurred him to go on without further coaxing.

"It began in a very simple way, Monsieur. We had a first conversation, in the course of which she uttered nothing but vague banalities. She, too, felt alone, at sea. She needed someone to extend a helping hand. Feeling that she was reticent about giving details, I asked for none and could only lavish on her the words of encouragement that apply to all cases. But I had surely found the right tone, for she asked me my name and begged me to answer her myself when she telephoned again. She did so the

147

next day, the day after that, and in the days following. I was only too glad to be of use to her. All my colleagues congratulated me when I told them of my new client. I felt that my *standing,* as you say in Europe, had considerably risen."

"No one was jealous? No one tried to take her away?"

"Monsieur, jealousy was unknown in the Service. We all rejoiced without the slightest ulterior motive over whatever good fortune might come to any one of us.

"That state of mind explains why M. Vincent—I still occupied a chair in his office facing him—refrained from asking questions about this client. Nor did I for several days ask him for advice, contrary to what I did in other cases, in which his experience always had been valuable to me.

"Nevertheless, after the latest conversation with the woman I decided to ask his help. Her agitation had troubled me. Now she complained incessantly about the cruelty of her husband and spoke more and more frequently of suicide.

" 'Cruelty of the husband,' M. Vincent said to me. 'A rather common case. I have had to treat similar ones and have often been able to initiate a cure. Let me consult my records.'

"He went to look for one of his notebooks in which, for years, he had set down the most remarkable facts of his career, along with appropriate comments. He had already shown me such records—a sort of repertory of human woes—with the method of compassion suitable to each. On several occasions I had seen his colleagues come to consult him on some thorny matter, and it was quite unusual for him not to find in his notebooks the solution to their problem.

"This time, however, after having rapidly run through the different cases classified under the heading: 'husband's cruelty,' he closed the notebook with a shake of the head.

" 'We don't have the necessary elements,' he said. 'Here there are only special cases. Try to learn something further about her in your next conversation. It would also be useful to me to hear this woman's voice, if you authorize me to. The voice is sometimes an essential index to steer you to the good path of compassion.'

"I accepted gratefully. I gave him an agreed-upon sign when my client called me that very evening. He pushed a button permitting him to hear our conversation. The woman seemed in the depths of depression.

" 'I tell you again, I can't stand any more. No, rest assured, I have no intention of killing myself. I don't even have the courage any longer. Following your advice, I tried with all my might to break through the shroud of loneliness. If only he would give a little of himself! A few minutes of attention in a day is all I ask. Even that's too much for him! The truth, Monsieur, is that I am married to a monster. I must explain to you . . . I'm not boring you?'

" 'You are not boring me in the least,' I said. 'I detect in you a distress by no means common. Don't hesitate to confide in me.'

" 'It's difficult to make you understand. Contempt, the need to cause suffering, mental cruelty. If you knew how my day is spent! This morning, for example . . .'

"She was silent, breathing with effort.

"I thought it useful to encourage her:

" 'That's right. We have ample time. Tell me about your day. I need precise facts to be able to counsel you usefully.'

"All the while I was speaking, I kept glancing at M. Vincent, to learn whether he approved of the way I was directing the conversation. Like me, he had adopted the listening posture. He made me a little sign with his finger that might pass for approval.

" 'This morning he got up at seven o'clock as he does every day. He walks stealthily. He pretends I don't hear him. In fact, he knows very well I'm not asleep. It isn't concern on his part that he is so quiet, it's to avoid kissing me before he leaves. I've tried getting up at the same time as he to prepare his breakfast. Never will he touch the food I set out for him. If I make coffee, he takes chocolate; if I prepare chocolate, he is satisfied with a slice of bread and butter. Ridiculous, I know. Pardon me for such details . . . but he does all this with the evident intention of wounding me. He leaves the house without having uttered a word. He runs away from me. He can't stand my presence any more. He is gone the whole day, sometimes for part of the night. I take my meals alone, always alone. When, for a wonder, he is there, it's worse. Not a kind word, not a friendly gesture, in spite of my overtures. Once I was bold enough—he frightens me—to ask him about his work. He raised his eyes to heaven with an exasperated look that bruised my spirit, a look of ruthless scorn meaning that his business couldn't possibly interest me. I sobbed over this for hours.'

"I'll be brief, Monsieur. This sad monologue continued for quite a long time. Trivial domestic sorrows. I had warned you that it was a case of despair, its causes banal. After she had finished, I spoke some pacifying words without much conviction, then I broke off the conversation, using the pretext of an urgent matter that had to be settled and making her promise to call back a few minutes later. As a matter fact, I wished to consult M. Vincent.

"Both he and I had hung up the phone with the same gesture, but he seemed reluctant to leave his position there in the hollow of the easy chair. His countenance was inscrutable. In the silence that dragged on, thinking of the woman who was soon going to call me back, I decided to attract his attention.

" 'M. Vincent, what do you think?' I asked.

"He came out of his reverie. He shrugged his shoulders and glared. He mumbled a few words impossible to make out. Then he looked at me, his geniality and serenity recovered . . .

" 'My young friend, to give you useful counsel is impossible. An odd case such as one meets with every now and then. I can do nothing for her. I recognized the voice. It is my wife.' "

# The
# Angelic
# Monsieur Edyh

# 1

*A* FRIEND OF MINE, Monsieur, lived through this experience. He was a school comrade with whom I had kept in close touch, though I went without news of him for long periods. Since our careers had followed different directions, we didn't frequent the same circles. I had taken my degree in law, as you know, and for a time had practiced at the bar—not too successfully—before entering upon a religious life. He had carried on his studies brilliantly in various branches of science with a passion for physics, biology, and the application of these disciplines to medical research. He had completed his studies in the finest universities of the Western world, presenting a doctoral dissertation, distinguished for great depth and

155

originality. When he came back to the Kingdom of Shandong, he carried on his profession but built up only a limited clientele, devoting the largest part of his time to
research, for which his unusually quick and penetrating
mind so well qualified him.

"In addition to his rigorous work, he had an interest
in the literature of different cultures, especially that of
the Anglo-Saxon. If I mention this fact, it is because the
reading of a British writer, quite well known, I believe,
was at the bottom of this strange adventure."

"Your fellow interests me, Old Man. This friend's
name?"

"It would grate on your ears and would be difficult to
translate into your tongue. If you're agreed, I'll call him
Jekyll."

"Jekyll? I've already read that name, Old Man. But
why Jekyll?"

"Quite simply because his adventures follow a path
similar to that of Stevenson's hero, though diverging
from it in many ways, and because it was the reading of
this novel that played a decisive role in his life. . . ."

"Old Man," I said, rubbing my hands together, "this
start seems to me promising. Then it was while reading
*The Strange Case of Doctor Jekyll and Mr. Hyde,* a novel
of which I am very fond, that your friend Dr. Jekyll . . ."

"My friend was strongly impressed by this book, for
not only did it correspond to his turn of mind, it followed
the very special direction he had given to research he was
secretly pursuing in his laboratory, research he deemed
on the point of success.

"He reread the work several times, and one day stopped

to brood over a certain passage that particularly struck him. I can cite it from memory, because the events that ensued spurred me, too, to reread the passage frequently and to question myself on its meaning."

"Quote it, Old Man, please do. Which passage?"

"This one, which is found in the confession of Dr. Jekyll himself. It is at the very instant when, swallowing for the first time the potion he had compounded, he gave birth to Hyde, the genius of evil.

" '*That night, I had come to the fatal crossroad. Had I approached my discovery in a more noble spirit, had I risked the experiment while under the empire of generous or pious aspirations, all must have been otherwise, and from these agonies of death and birth I had come forth an angel instead of a fiend.*'

"Monsieur, these considerations were extremely important to my friend for, as I've told you, he was convinced that his research had led him to the brink of a prodigious discovery, and the events that followed proved he was not deluding himself. He had rediscovered the composition of a drink making it possible to divide a human being into two, physically and morally, and to isolate in one of the structures all the good or all the evil, whose complex intermingling in himself tormented him just as it disturbed Stevenson's hero. You can readily understand how this passage caused him to reflect and what uneasiness it inspired about the crucial experiment he was on the verge of trying on himself."

"I understand his qualms," I said thoughtfully. "All the good or all the evil!"

"Just that, according to the mental disposition of the

157

experimenter at the moment of putting it to the test; my friend had good reasons for being convinced that the Jekyll of the novel had seen rightly on this point.

"My friend, Monsieur, aside from his intellectual capacities, which were exceptional, was an average man physically as well as morally, neither better nor worse than most. And the clear perception he had of his own nature plunged him into deep anxiety. Conscientious and objective, he was obliged to confess that his research had been inspired much more by scientific curiosity— perhaps, after all, a morbid curiosity—than by a noble ideal. To try the experiment while he was in this state of mind was to risk giving birth to a hideous monster, and being devoured by all the vices like Stevenson's Mr. Hyde. This prospect haunted him day and night and made him shudder, all the more because he was on the point of marrying a young woman of great beauty, whom he adored and who returned his love. To cause her to run the risk of any contact whatsoever with a monster of that sort seemed to him an abomination. Thus he resolved to put off the moment of making the leap and came to ask my advice. He had confidence in my judgment and knew he could count on my discretion.

"The religion of Doubt, which I profess, prohibited me from expressing a definitive opinion on the moral value of his project, but the danger that had become apparent to him seemed to me very real, and I could only strengthen him in his determination to delay the experiment. I advised him to reflect further, to flee from the world, to abstain from every malicious or dubious thought, to make a sort of meditative retreat, at the end of which he should question himself with the greatest sincerity on his spiritual bearings and to try the venture only after he was certain this orientation was toward the good. Then the creature so begotten could only be adorned with all the virtues. He promised me to follow my wise and prudent advice, and we parted.

"I didn't see him again for quite a long time, but he subsequently told me he had kept his word. He led an exemplary and edifying life, summoning all his will and energy to exorcise the forces of evil that, at moments, tried to take possession of his mind, as they try to in each and every one of us. He made retreat after retreat, observed fasts, abstinence, mortification of the flesh, even flagellation, busying himself with works of charity and spending the rest of his time in meditation. During this period of moral preparation he gave important business abroad as a pretext for postponing his marriage and separating himself from his fiancée."

"Are you sure that this ascetic life is the best way to banish evil, Old Man?"

"It brought positive results, Monsieur, as you'll see. After several weeks of this regimen my friend had a kind of revelation, the sudden and brilliant conviction that his mind was finally oriented toward the good alone, that there no longer existed any disturbing thought in his project—simply the noble ambition to give birth to a being endowed with all the virtues, to an angel, as the famous passage of Stevenson suggested. Freed from his scruples and no longer having any reason to vacillate, he entered his laboratory that very evening and, after a final moment of hesitation, swallowed the potion in one gulp, the formula for which he had brought to perfection after years of work."

"Your story appeals to me, Old Man," I said. "For once, it doesn't wound my sensibility. The birth of an angel in this world is a pleasant prospect. Why do you stop?"

"Because, Monsieur, I must make a break in my narrative. As I have told you, I didn't see Dr. Jekyll again during this period of preparation. It was only much later, and in the manner you will see, that I learned he had decided to put the great venture to the test. Moreover, I hadn't attached very much importance to our last conversation. In spite of the respect my friend's scientific genius inspired in me, I couldn't help thinking in the depths of my being that he was deluding himself about the reality of his so-called discovery. A physical doubling of the personality seemed to me like the dream of a novelist desperately tracking down an original idea and taking refuge in extravagant imaginings to break the iron collar of the commonplace. Some people act this way at times, Monsieur."

"Why do you stare at me like that, Old Man? Continue. In your place, I believe I should have been as skeptical as you."

"Well, I seldom thought any more of our conversation. I ascribed the declarations of my friend to a bout of fever that occasionally torments the best minds after too much work. Then, one day, I was visited by an unknown man who forced me to change my mind.

"This young man—he seemed hardly more than twenty —presented himself with the utmost civility, like a

160

stranger descended of a rich family traveling the world to complete his education. Having heard so well of me, he said, he wished to make my acquaintance.

"Listening to this preamble, delivered with the greatest courtesy and an exquisite grace, I couldn't help but be greatly astonished. I led a life of unostentatious retirement, and if, like all men of religion, those of Doubt being no exception, I exerted myself to perform a little good around me, I was not presumptuous enough to imagine that my virtues, modest as they were, had been held up as an example in the realm of Shandong, much less in a foreign land.

"As he continued to speak in this vein, making me blush by his undeserved compliments, I observed the unknown man minutely, not yet understanding the real purpose of his visit. The moment he entered I had been captivated by the fineness of his features, the softness of his voice, the nobility of his bearing, and, above all, by the special character of a smile stamped with kindness. The more closely I looked at him, the surer I felt that I was talking to a being of rare and refined essence. He was unusually tall, but so admirably proportioned that his stature was not disturbing. His garments were simple, but he wore them with such distinction that they appeared rich and elegant."

"Hurry up, Old Man," I murmured impatiently. "I've guessed."

"You are very sharp, Monsieur, and I haven't meant to pose an enigma. I would have guessed, as you have, if there had been the least trait in this individual, the tiniest expression reminiscent of my friend Jekyll, the

161

doctor. But this was not the case. So I continued to listen to him, perplexed, until he came to the real object of his visit.

" 'I presume,' he said, 'that like everywhere else in the world, there is great misery to be relieved in this town.'

" 'You can be sure of that, Mon . . . Monsieur.'

"I was so greatly impressed by his bearing and his manner that, despite his youth, I was on the point of calling him Monseigneur.

" 'And I assume you know many unfortunate people who are worthy of compassion.'

" 'Each day I pass by people in frightful destitution without, alas, being able to help them. Like most pastors, I share with the poor the few alms I receive from the rich, but it's a drop of water in the ocean.'

" 'That's just what I've been thinking,' he said with a sigh, 'and that's the reason I am allowing myself to ask your help. May I ask you as a service to give them this money, but, above all, without indicating it comes from me?'

"This, Monsieur, consisted of bundle after bundle of bank notes. Chatting all the while, he took them out of a valise he had deposited near him on his arrival. I rubbed my eyes, I caught my breath. When he had finished, there was an impressive heap on my table, and at a glance I saw that these notes were the largest denomination of the kingdom—a sum such as I had never had in my possession or even contemplated having. I was so dumbfounded that at first I had difficulty in expressing my thanks. This gift seemed too handsome to be real.

"The unknown man smiled, as if he read my thoughts.

" 'I can assure you there's no question of counterfeit money,' he said. 'These notes came straight from the bank. I give you my word on it.'

"Again I stammered:

" 'I don't know how to thank you in the name of the destitute. For it's to them the whole of this princely gift will go.'

" 'I don't doubt it for a second,' he said with a broader smile, a smile very remarkable, strange, truly angelic, in the common phrase that came instinctively to mind as I looked at him admiringly.

" 'I suppose I ought to give you a receipt,' I murmured, not yet fully recovered from my surprise.

" 'There's no need of that. I know you and that's why I've chosen you for this mission.'

" 'You know me?'

"He didn't answer but just smiled again, nodding his head. Only at this moment, Monsieur, less perspicacious than you, confronted with the strangeness of the personage and his incomprehensible, almost not human, comportment, did I have an intuition of what you divined some time ago. I looked him in the eye.

" 'Monsieur, may I ask you your name?'

" 'From you, my friend,' he said, lowering his voice, 'I have no reason to conceal it. You have known me under the name of Jekyll. But today, call me Edyh. It's the name I've chosen.'

" 'It is not possible!' I cried out. 'You are trying to deceive me. Such demonic practices in these times, in the realm of Shandong! I can't believe you.'

" 'I'm going to bring forward the proof,' he replied

163

calmly. 'It's important that someone should be able to witness the authenticity of this marvelous discovery later on. Although it costs me some effort, I'm going to assume before you my old, heavy trappings. Dr. Jekyll also has obligations.'

"Monsieur, I was then witness to a scene described several times in Stevenson's book and depicted by several generations of film-makers. The unknown man—should I still call him unknown?—asked me to bring him a glass. Then he took out of the bottom of his valise two flasks and a test tube, poured into the glass two doses of minutely measured liquids, carefully mixed the draught, which began to boil up and from which a whitish vapor escaped, and swallowed it in one gulp. I asked myself whether I was not the victim of hallucination.

"I shall try not to prolong the description of the following scene. There again, I thought I was still dreaming and tried to persuade myself that the sight of the man, gasping and writhing under my eyes was only the nightmarish memory of scenes from a film. This sort of agony lasted some minutes, at the end of which the spasms progressively disminished. At the same time the height of the man was shrinking and he aged under my eyes by several years. His face lost that angelic sweetness that had so captivated me, and his features changed. In short, Monsieur, the being I now had before me, still haggard and panting, was none other than my friend Dr. Jekyll, a composite creature, molded of both good and bad, neither handsome nor ugly, rendered a little bit ridiculous at that moment by clothes that had been made for a man a good half foot taller than he and that now appeared like cheap finery, since they were no longer enhanced by the manners of the angel Edyh.

"I was not dreaming. After having recovered his calm a little. Dr. Jekyll reassured me by taking my hand and addressing me in a voice I knew well.

" 'Forgive me, my friend,' he said, 'for having made you witness to a scene that must be painful to watch. You must believe it's equally so for me, and I don't resort to it except from necessity. But I had to resume my original personality. Curiously enough, the change from Jekyll to Edyh is infinitely less painful; moreover, I don't know why. May I ask you to have one of my outfits brought from my place so I may return to my lodgings without attracting the attention of passers-by in this attire?'

"I deferred until later his fuller explanation. I myself went to his home, which was not very far from mine. I invented an excuse to get his servant to give me some clothes, the servant being a bit feeble-minded and apparently accustomed to the rather whimsical ways of his master. When I returned home, I found Jekyll prey to a meditation that seemed a little disquieting, his head in his hands, his look fixed on the bank notes heaped on my table.

" 'Jekyll,' I said, trying to jest in order to mask my emotion, 'I don't know whether this is witchcraft or the last word in science, but I'm sure the poor devils whose misfortune I'll be able to relieve, thanks to Edyh's generosity, wouldn't be tormented by this question even if they knew the nature of their benefactor.'

"He gave a start and the hint of anxiety I thought I had discerned in his face seemed to grow more intense.

" 'Do you have any idea of the sum he brought you after having cashed a check at the bank signed in my name?'

" 'I can only estimate that the alms are princely.'

" 'Princely—how right you are,' he said with a touch of bitterness. 'I know the total myself, for I have a memory of all the acts and thoughts of my double, that angel of generosity.'

"He mentioned a sizable figure, as I had foreseen, and remained silent once more, hesitant.

" 'Listen, Jekyll,' I said after a moment's reflection, 'I sense your reticence. I don't know whether or not I have the right to accept this gift for the poor of my parish.'

" 'Do you really feel that way?' he cried with a sudden vivacity.

" 'Unless you confirm to me—you, Dr. Jekyll—that you concur in the munificence of Edyh. After all, this money comes from your bank account.'

" 'That's true,' he assented. 'All this is mine.'

"I was aware that he was becoming more and more unhappy and taciturn.

" 'Don't you find he has exaggerated a little?' he asked in a low voice.

" 'His point of view is that of an angel of generosity. It isn't inevitably yours or mine, unworthy creature that I am.'

" 'But if I took the money back, I'm afraid he would harbor resentment toward me.'

" 'Edyh must be incapable of rancor,' I remarked. 'He is an angel.'

"He seemed touched by this logic and finally came to a decision.

" 'Give me back just half of it,' he said with a sigh. 'The amount is really excessive. It is almost ostentatious.'

"We counted the bundles. We divided them into two equal parts, and he put one back in his suitcase. Enough remained on the table to accomplish great good. Meanwhile, as he was changing his clothes, he told me the circumstances of his transformation, which I have already related to you. Then he asked me to excuse him, alleging it was urgent for Dr. Jekyll to go look after his affairs. Before leaving me, he made this request:

" 'If, by chance, Edyh returns with the same charitable intentions, I beg you, my friend, try to make him listen to reason. What the devil, generosity must be kept within certain limits!'

"I promised I would, and he went away shaking his head."

"I detect some unforeseen situations, Old Man," I interrupted.

"You couldn't be more correct, Monsieur. Unforeseen and even tragic from a certain point of view."

"However, the beginning had led me to hope for happy developments. The birth of an angel ought to be considered an auspicious event."

"That's exactly what I thought then and what Dr. Jekyll hoped. He had miraculously realized his ambition. Without question, thanks to the austere life he had led before performing the experiment and to the right-mindedness and high moral worth he had striven to attain, he was in the state of angelic purity when he brought about his transformation, and it was actually an angelic creature who came forth into the world, a creature molded of pure angelic feelings and possessing within itself an almost infinite capacity for angelic acts.

"But to make you live through the cascade of unanticipated events more fully I will read you a document that came into my possession a long while after the facts I've reported to you. It was drawn up by Jekyll himself, who, again like Stevenson's hero, had experienced the need to make a sort of confession. Monsieur, I don't have it with me. I'll bring it to you tomorrow evening. You'll have to be patient till then, for I must refresh my memory."

Old scamp! I thought. One more of your tricks to prolong the suspense . . . "At your command, Old Man. I shall be here tomorrow at the same time. Don't make me wait too long."

## 2

My nocturnal storyteller kept me eagerly awaiting him for just under an hour and condescended to pick up the thread of his narrative the moment he arrived.

"Here is the document, Monsieur," he said, putting a scroll of yellowed paper on the table. "It was intended for me. It was brought to me by a passer-by who had found it under the window of Dr. Jekyll's laboratory. I am going to read you some passages. These will give you an exact account of the facts. But what creates their chief interest is that they illustrate the way in which the principal personage was affected by them—or by the personages, I should say, for though the text was begun and edited in large part by Jekyll, it seems that Edyh inserted some notes of his own when he was brought into being."

"Read on, Old Man, I'm curious to know the secrets and reactions of these two heroes, or, rather, of this double hero."

"I'll pass over the first part. In it Jekyll sets forth the details of his research, his ambition, hopes, virtuous preparation after reading the passage in Stevenson I cited, his first transformation into an angel, the visit of Edyh to me, and his return to the form of Jekyll. There is nothing there you don't already know. Here he is, leaving my home; I read his words:

"*'After having recovered a part of the extravagant gift made by Edyh, I couldn't fend off a muted anxiety. I possess, of course, a rather handsome fortune, but it should not be tapped too often. Such thoughts were running through my mind while returning home, but they were thoughts mingled with remorse. Don't forget, my friend, that I myself am a composite being, an amalgam of good and evil. While the bad element deplored the significant loss I had borne, the good regretted having taken back half of these alms. I knew that the angel, now vanished, would reproach me for my avarice and egoism. This mingling of disparate feelings plunged me into great confusion.*

"*'A confusion so disagreeable that I resolved to give myself a little time before making a new experiment, to remain for the present Dr. Jekyll, while reflecting on all the possible implications of my discovery, some of which hadn't occurred to me up to this time.*

*" 'This is what I did for a fortnight. I had resumed my practice, my habitual occupations, in other words, a mixture of actions and thoughts neither good nor bad, but making it a point of honor, even so, to emphasize the good —a little; rationally. With my fiancée I had drawn tighter the bonds of affection that had grown lax because of my experiment, and I had succeeded in winning her forgiveness for my neglect, without, of course, revealing the cause.*

*" 'My friend, at the end of two weeks I could stand it no longer. The temptation was too strong. I experienced the insurmountable desire to become angelic again. I was harassed, tyrannized over day and night by a thirst for absolute good. A second time I drank the potion. Again I became Edyh.'*

"The temptation of the good was too strong, Monsieur. Have you grasped this? I see your thoughts wandering and you are listening with only half an ear."

"I've understood perfectly, Old Man. Go ahead. Then he became Edyh again."

"And I saw him appear once more in that form. But let me read you what follows in this document, written in the same hand as Jekyll's, a little more carefully. The thought and style are different from the beginning. It's clear that it is one of those passages in which Edyh holds the pen."

"And Dr. Jekyll allowed them to survive?"

"Doubtless, in his desire to unveil the whole truth, he didn't wish to suppress them. Perhaps, too, one must see in this his intention to put others on guard, addressing those who might have it in their power to be tempted to follow his example. He would have wished to reveal all the purity of soul of the angel and its surprising consequences. Whatever the case, here is what Edyh said when newly re-embodied:

" *'At last, here I am, become an angel again. The transformation was brought about this time without the least malaise, almost with pleasure. I feel light, trembling with joy at being delivered from evil, the evil that often causes Jekyll to go astray. I pity him with all my heart, but I must be on the alert for his reactions and machinations when he awakes. I shall take care not to let his egoism thwart my charitable impulses. I have gone to withdraw funds that will allow me to lighten the burden of a few poor people: a considerable sum—not enough, alas! for all the good I burn to accomplish. But too large a check would risk arousing the suspicions of the bank. Already, just as before, his signature occasioned a minute verification; but it was flawless. Then I shall act from now on so Jekyll cannot take away a part of my alms from the suffering needy. I shall not take on his form until the good is accomplished. Irreparable.'* "

The Old Man interrupted his reading, took off the spectacles he had put on, and commented:

"*Irreparable,* Monsieur. This adjective is odd from the hand of Edyh. Do you suppose it escaped him inadvertently? I believe it more likely that Jekyll, taking up the document later, added it himself, and with a certain irritability, if not rage, for it is badly written. In any case, the term is quite suggestive.

**171**

"As he states, Edyh then took precautions. He came to find me with his valise stuffed with bank notes. He made the same remarks as on his first visit, but added, smiling, that he hoped this time to make the rounds of the destitute with me and not to leave me until the distribution was finished.

"Recalling my friend's attitude and his recommendations, I began by refusing curtly, alleging that the money belonged to Dr. Jekyll and that I had no right to deprive him of it. Edyh didn't become the least bit angry and began to talk over the situation with me methodically, showing much patience—the veritable patience of an angel.

"Monsieur, you just can't conceive how futile it is to make objections to an angel who has taken it into his head to do good. Angels have a logic and dialectic all their own before which one is obliged to lower his lance. He advanced such convincing arguments, punctuated with such touching smiles, that he succeeded in convincing me of Jekyll's avarice and my own coldness of heart. After all, it isn't right for a man of religion to refuse alms destined for his poor. I yielded and in his company undertook to make the rounds of those whom I knew to be the neediest. At the end of the day, the valise was empty and we had filled a good many wretched homes with happiness. A last smile lighted up his angelic face, and he took leave of me with many thanks for my cooperation. I myself felt light-hearted. I don't know, Monsieur, whether you have felt that exalting joy one experiences in doing good."

"Good that doesn't cost you yourself a penny," I remarked. "And Jekyll?"

"His reaction was what one might suppose, but recriminations would have served no purpose. The good had been done. I didn't even see him appear, as I feared he might, to reproach me for my weakness. But let me resume my reading. It's still Edyh speaking:

"*'After I had ended my rounds with the saintly man, my most urgent duty accomplished, I decided to put on Jekyll's habit again. I didn't resign myself to this without a certain repugnance. I felt much better in my skin than in his, my conscience clear and freed of all its guilts. Furthermore, the change from Edyh to Jekyll becomes a little more painful physically each time. (Is it just because of this repugnance?) But I ought to assure good service to my clientele, if it were only to nourish our bank account. And, too, I can't help thinking of Jekyll's fiancée and feeling sorry for her. I can't face the prospect of the grief she would feel if he disappeared in me forever, without leaving a trace. I am so constituted that knowledge of the suffering of others is unbearable to me. Thus, again it's because of goodness and generosity that I shut myself in my laboratory to drink the potion once more. As I feared, during the transformation I suffered the pangs of death, intensified by those of birth.*

"*'During the transformation I suffered the pangs of death, intensified by those of birth . . .'*"

"You're repeating yourself, Old Man."

"No, Monsieur, it's Jekyll changing the guard. Here he is, rising up and speaking in his turn:

" '. . . and, the miracle consummated once more, a terrible anguish has taken the place of physical pain. I was present, powerless, at the squandering of my fortune. I knew that Edyh had many more follies in mind to allay the misfortunes of others with the help of my money. It was becoming impossible for me to let him do it. I had to make a painful, yet indispensable, resolution if I wished to escape total ruin. This time I decided to renounce forever these experiences and I swore on the head of the person I hold dearest in the world, on the head of my fiancée, never again to bring forth Edyh.

" 'I have kept my word. I have never taken the fatal drink again to bring on the metamorphosis. But then, my good friend, an incident occurred bordering on the amazing, which plunged me into the most terrible anguish, making me fully realize the imprudence I had committed by releasing the occult forces that control our organisms.

" 'It was wintertime, the harsh winter you've just lived through. I was walking on the shores of our lake, which was completely frozen over. The bank was deserted. I was reflecting on past events and congratulating myself on my decision, which I now knew to be irrevocable. Then as I was thinking of the sweet face of my fiancée, our approaching marriage and all the reasons I had for being happy, I suddenly saw two urchins playing on the ice. I hardly had time to realize how risky it was, and before I could call out to them to get back to solid ground, the accident I feared happened. The ice gave way suddenly under the weight of one of the boys and he disappeared in a hole of water. I looked around in search of help.

174

## The Angelic Monsieur Edyh

*There was nobody. The cold had chased away strollers.
I called out; no echo answered my calls. I had the fleeting
impulse to go to the aid of the child myself, an impulse
very quickly restrained. A moment of reflection was
enough for me to calculate that it would be pure madness.
The ice, which had proved too thin to hold up a small
boy's weight, would certainly break under mine. I was
sure to drown if the water was deep, for, you see, my
friend, I don't know how to swim. At best, lung congestion lay in wait for me, fatal to my bronchi, which are
delicate.*

*" 'I opened my mouth in renewed calls for help and
the incident I've mentioned happened at this very moment, an incident like the one that overwhelmed Stevenson's character. I felt from the signs I knew well that the
transformation was beginning—starting spontaneously,
against my will, without the help of any drug. I scarcely
had time to ask in anguish what new trick Edyh was going
to play on me. I was already putting on his psychic
uniform. . . . Ah! Does one reflect at moments like
this? I certainly lost no time weighing the danger. I
rushed onto the ice to the rescue of the child.' "*

"This is becoming incoherent, Old Man!"

"Why no, Monsieur, it's Edyh who again takes up the
account. I'll sum up what follows this passage, since it
has hardly anything of interest. The ice gave way under
the angel's weight, as the prudent Jekyll had foreseen.
Luckily, the water wasn't very deep at this spot and Edyh
was only up to his armpits. Half wading, half crawling on
the ice, he was able to get to the child and pull him onto
the bank, with the help of passers-by whom the shouts of

175

*The Marvelous Palace*

Jekyll and the second urchin had finally alerted. With great difficulty Edyh escaped the witnesses' praise and got back to his home, where fever soon laid him low. He barely had time to drink the magic potion before taking to his bed, stricken with a bad pulmonary congestion, which kept him suspended between life and death for a week and in bed for more than a month. Here are his reflections, which he began to jot down as soon as he had recovered his spirits:

" '*It seems to me I'm coming out of a long night peopled with bad dreams. Alas! They were not dreams, I know it only too well. In spite of all my efforts at resistance, the moulting came about spontaneously and I feel this drama is in danger of being repeated at any instant. The angel Edyh materialized at the sight of a human being in distress. He couldn't resist the desire to fly to his aid. He is senseless. Not for one second did he think of the danger he made me run. I have narrowly escaped with my life. My health is precarious and it will take me months to recover, provided he doesn't play some new trick on me of his own devising. I am now at the mercy of his virtuous impulses. I will have to exert every effort to shun the vicinity of human distress, to avoid at all costs the slightest occasion for coming to the rescue of some unfortunate being who could still release him in spite of me.*'

"Here, Monsieur, is another passage I'll summarize for you. It appears that Edyh didn't show himself anymore for a rather long time. Jekyll's tactic seemed crowned with success. He carefully avoided association with the needy, with all those who might have launched an appeal for help, and he sought the company only of happy people. This required him to be constantly alert, which was trying at times, but the result was worth the trouble. He spent long hours in his fiancée's company, making preparations for the wedding, which was to take place in the near future, persuading himself that life with her would help him cast off once and for all this phantom of an angel.

"But this was to reckon without Edyh, Monsieur. He manifested himself anew, spontaneously, and the fact, in a sense, of having been kept chained up for weeks had made him more impetuous than ever in his will to do good. Listen to him. He now takes up the pen and will not soon let go of it. I observe, too, that he describes his sensations with great self-satisfaction, as though he were intoxicated by the perfume of his virtues. In any case, he makes us perceive, as well as do the lamentations of his double, the tragedy of the situation in which my unhappy friend is caught:

" '*At last, here I am incarnated anew. Jekyll was holding me captive, evincing a certain Machiavellianism, fleeing from every outstretched hand, receiving only the wealthy with slight illnesses, no longer seeing anyone but his fiancée. To live this dream of happiness with her is a condition devoid of all interest to me, leaving me completely indifferent. It is pure chance that has allowed me to outwit his ruses and come to my senses: the fortuitous encounter along a winding path with a leprous woman, at the very moment he was strolling in the country, arm in arm, with his fiancée.*

" '*Her presence didn't prevent a thing. In vain he*

*clasped her convulsively to him as soon as he felt the first symptoms of the transformation and attempted to lead her away. It was too late; once again the impelling force of the good to be accomplished was irresistible. Of course, I regretted the terror that this moulting taking place in her arms caused the young girl. To feel so very close to her, against her own body, a beloved being suddenly increase in height by half a foot, to see his features change, and an instant later to behold a different man is undoubtedly a trying experience for a fiancée, even if the new man is younger, more handsome, and more open in countenance than her betrothed. I would have wished to spare her this trial. I tried to reassure her by my smile, but she didn't leave me time and fled howling. Seeing her thus half crazed with fear, I had a moment's hesitation —only a moment's—then I gave up trying to catch her. I had something far better to do than to console her.*

*" 'The leper was there, she who had snatched me from my lethargy by her mere appearance. She was known in the countryside and I still reproach myself for not having thought of her sooner. How was it that I had not been moved to pity before by her sad fate? A girl still very young, afflicted with disease from her childhood, who lived in a tumbledown cabin in the woods, crushed by misery and terrible isolation. The town folk out for a stroll and the peasants avoided the neighborhood of her cabin. She survived by eating food the town administration ordered deposited every day at a suitable spot in the forest, after having forbidden her to frequent places of habitation. This day, she had ventured exceptionally far from her reserved territory, impelled by a presenti-*

*ment, a dream she confessed to me later when we had become intimate, that had made her anticipate a miraculous event. Blessed be this dream! It gave me the chance to bring a little warmth and hope into the existence of a being who needed them so much.*

*" 'The leprous girl had reacted neither to the transformation to which she had been witness nor to the terrified flight and cries of the fiancée. She looked at me insistently. I, in turn, watched her attentively and was able to convince myself of her physical decay. Her face was extremely ugly. If leprosy hadn't yet reached its final stage, the one that devours and putrefies the flesh, this hideous eating away of the body was quite enough to excite my pity and compassion.*

*" 'I smiled at her, putting all the goodness of my soul into the smile to compensate for the rather ridiculous spectacle I must have presented in Jekyll's clothes, now become too tight. She responded to this sign of friendship by a frightful grimace of her swollen face. I opened my arms to her. She drew near. I pressed her to my heart and gave her a brotherly kiss. I felt her throb and melt in a great burst of gratitude. For me it was the most moving recompense my soul had ever experienced.*

*" 'Heaven had put us in each other's presence: heaven would not separate us again. I felt that this fortuitous meeting would allow me to surpass myself and attain the limits of the sublime. I told her I was an angel, sent to this earth to dedicate myself, and was ready for any sacrifice to better her lot. She thanked me in a slightly raucous voice, with tears in her eyes, eyes that alone gave a human touch to a ravaged face. To my question: Apart*

179

*from your illness, to which I can bring no great remedy, alas, what is most painful to you in your condition? she replied without hesitation: Solitude. I shall die of it before dying of leprosy.*

" '*I love you, I said immediately. When this cry burst forth from my heart, I knew a divine moment. My decision had been made in an instant. I would never leave her. I would persuade her that she was desirable, that I adored her. I felt a sacred mission to make her know all the joys of love, which until then had been denied her.*

" '*I love you, I declared again, and I didn't hesitate this time to plant a lover's kiss on her repellant lips. She didn't respond, but the trembling of her body sent a thrill of pleasure through me. Ah, how I pity Jekyll, who will never know such delights.*

" '*I put my arm around her waist and accompanied her as far as her hut, a foul dilapidated dwelling, the sight of which made my heart bleed. All this is going to change, I said to her. I wish a different setting for you, one in which you'll be able to flower. I told her that I had to settle certain urgent affairs in order to be able to consecrate myself entirely to her and begged her to wait for me there, to think of me, to believe that I would come back the next day, never to leave her again. A shade of distress darkened her face, but I smiled at her and she understood at once that I was incapable of lying.*

" '*I tore myself from her arms to put into operation the plan I had just conceived. Then I went to the room I rented under the name Edyh, to put on suitable clothes. After that, I went to Jekyll's home. I knew the house was empty. His old servant had died a few days earlier and he hadn't yet found a replacement. I had a clear field. I made a clean sweep of all the jewels and precious objects in his apartment. I emptied the coffers that contained several bags of gold pieces, hoarded out of avarice. I carried the lot of it to my furnished room, biding my time to convert these useless treasures into cash as I went along, since I foresaw that my needs were going to be considerable. Next I went to the bank and withdrew a very large sum of cash. This time the banker didn't bother to verify the signature. Since Dr. Jekyll had not challenged the preceding checks, the banker, though he might have been astonished, had no real reason to create difficulties.*

*" 'Then I disposed of the tidy fortune indispensable to the realization of my project. I got in touch with one of the town's best architects and described the kind of dwelling in which I had decided to lodge the leper: a palace. Nothing seemed to me to be too beautiful, too luxurious, for this poor girl. I also wanted it to be built in the shortest possible time.*

*" 'The architect, too, was astonished at my demands and at first was hesitant. The funds I declared I was ready to turn over to him on the spot began to shake him. The way I pleaded my case finally won him over. I should mention here that the nobility of my bearing and the smile with which I instinctively knew how to grace discussions generally smoothed away all the resistant whims of my interlocutors. I early had perceived that no one was capable of questioning my perfect uprightness after having looked at me for a few moments. Further, I did not hide from the architect the object I had in mind: to*

*transform the sordid existence of a wretched woman by bringing her luxury, as if with the rub of a good fairy's ring. Once more, then, I was able to find the right arguments to touch a heart and succeeded in convincing the man he was acting for the good over and beyond transacting excellent business. He promised to begin work the very next day, at the site I indicated to him, not far from the miserable hovel in which the leper was wasting away.*

*" 'That done, I settled certain formalities necessary to the pursuit of my plan, then I returned to her. The smile that lighted up her face at my arrival paid me amply for the trouble I had taken. It was a real smile and no longer a grimace. Already, love was transforming her. I knew you would come back, she said to me. For always, I replied, clasping her in my arms. I adore you. We are going to be married tomorrow. I have made all the arrangements."*

"Monsieur, Edyh continues to hold forth in this way for quite some time, and I'd better just sum up the end of this passage. I must tell you that he kept his word and married the leprous woman, whose very appearance put all men to flight. He described their odd honeymoon with many details, expatiating gratuitously on the joy he gives this woman and on the satisfaction he draws from it himself. With equal enthusiasm he depicts the palace he is having built for her. As he had demanded, one wing was completed very rapidly, in which they were soon able to settle, there to shelter their love. Since the cost of this edifice exceeded his estimates, he had to liquidate what remained of Jekyll's fortune to satisfy his taste for perfection. That work of art was entirely completed at the end of some months, a palace of a thousand and one nights, it seems, and according to his statements it appears the couple knew an unclouded happiness."

"And had many children, perhaps," I protested. "Old Man, your story takes on the air of a fairy tale. Is it to please children?"

"A fairy tale that ended quite badly, Monsieur. Edyh should have been able so to end his days, steeped in the good and without taking again the form of Jekyll. Moreover, he had this firm intention, but it came about that one day he was compelled to act differently. Listen to him again:

" '*I was hoping to remain an angel and never to become Dr. Jekyll again, a being over whom evil has too great a hold, but a new encounter changed my destiny, obliging me to reflect on past events and see them in a different light.*

" '*I was alone. I had left my beloved wife for an evening, curious to see again the town in which I was twice born. I walked the length of the ramparts without daring to enter the inner city—I don't too well know why— when I caught sight of a woman who was coming toward me. I was troubled by the melancholy of her face. She came still closer and I was even more distressed at recognizing in her Dr. Jekyll's unhappy fiancée.*

" '*Unhappy indeed, oh how intensely so! She was walking with her head lowered. Everything about her, both the way her features had shriveled and the beclouded brow and the furrows tears had made in her cheeks gave witness that she was crushed by boundless grief. This girl was clearly the unhappiest creature in the world, and I was the one—I, Edyh—who had caused her suffering!*

" 'Immediately I felt myself burning with desire to come to her aid. When she passed me, I attracted her attention by coughing and used my wonted weapon: my most angelic smile. It had no effect on her. Quite the contrary. She raised her eyes and looked at me. Did she recognize the person who in the past had taken her fiancé's place in her arms? Very likely. My face doubtless recalled a memory of horror. She jumped, let out an exclamation, and fled, as she had done months before.*

" 'I stayed where I was, crushed in turn. I wasn't used to such a rebuff. What could I do? Someone was dreadfully unhappy because of me and for the first time in my existence I was powerless to help.*

" 'I didn't return home. I spent the night walking around the town, reflecting on this situation, intolerable for an angel. I reached the conclusion that only Jekyll could allay her sorrow by coming before her. In the early hours this duty seemed to me inevitable. I had to bring Dr. Jekyll back to life.'*

"And that's what he does, Monsieur. There he is, returning to the doctor's home, entering the laboratory, and swallowing the draught. I pass over the scene of transformation, always the same, yet more and more painful, and here is my friend Jekyll, who takes up the account."

"I suppose we are going to hear a lot of laments."

"No question about it, Monsieur."

"Old Man, your story is tragic, even loathsome in certain respects, but I can't resist being amused at moments, and I'm annoyed with myself."

"Don't be the least bit ashamed, Monsieur. My religion professes that tragedy and farce are often intimately related. Here, then, is Jekyll:

" '*I return to my wretched existence in the laboratory adjoining my empty, shabby office, where I haven't so much as a chair to sit on. Not a bed, not a cushion. Mad man, criminal that I was for letting loose that angel. Aside from his sickening virtue, he is the most stupid of creatures who ever haunted heaven, earth, or hell. He has set free my personality, hoping I would console my fiancée. How could I lift my eyes toward her today? How would I dare even approach her when I feel in my flesh the first gnawings of leprosy? What kind of life could I offer her now that I'm despoiled of everything? Edyh has wasted my fortune, sold all my furniture, to build and decorate the palace of his dreams. That wasn't enough for him. He had to have money and still more money to comfort other and yet other kinds of misery. Then, my friend, do you know what he did? In my hand, he signed checks for very large sums without cash to cover them.*

" '*So now prison awaits me. I shall end my days either there or in a leper colony. Abandoned, ruined, sick, dishonored—that's the abject state to which that angel has reduced me. Today I am the unhappiest of men.*

" '*The unhappiest of men. O God, what cry of distress have I let escape! Hardly had I uttered it when I felt in my body the symptoms that have never deceived me. It is Edyh who is coming back, Edyh, who can't resist the appeal of misery. I am growing tall. I am becoming good. Help! . . .*'

" '*. . . I am tortured by remorse. What to do, what to*

185

*do to comfort the terrible suffering of poor Jekyll? I see a single solution. Relieve him of my person, which poisons his existence. Let Edyh disappear forever! . . .*

" ' *. . . What torture. Now, in turn, I am becoming Jekyll again without absorbing the drug. And this monster has swallowed poison without thinking, without even suspecting that he was doing away with me at the same time as himself. O! would that I had given him intelligence at the same time as the instinct for charity! I had neglected that aspect of the problem at the time of my moral preparation. This poison is unrelenting, I know. There remain scarcely a few minutes of respite to deplore the criminality of the angel, to attest that for the first time the transformation of Edyh into me came about spontaneously and that it is in the guise of Dr. Jekyll that I die cursing him.*

" 'With my hand already cold I sign this confession, which is addressed to you, my good friend, and I throw it out the window, hoping it will reach you.*"

"There you have it, Monsieur. Here ends this strange document, for the authenticity of which I can warrant, for I was witness to many of the facts it relates. Having read it, I immediately went to my friend's lodgings. I found his lifeless body there in the setting he has described, where, just as in Stevenson's novel, a vial still containing some drops of a fatal poison was found open at his side.

"Only a few details of no importance, Monsieur, remain to be added. Dr. Jekyll's betrothed went mad with grief and had to be shut up in an asylum. As for the leper in the palace, she died of sorrow and despair in the solitude now come upon her again."

"You didn't have to mention those details, Old Man," I said with rancor. "I had guessed them. I have learned to know you well."